Overlord
Penguin Books

The outcome of the last great war has shaped the lives of a whole generation – but it is a generation which has only experienced the chaos, cruelty and uncertainty of those years through the media. Direct knowledge would be impossible, but even now books and films continue to hack out the same old fantasies: blood and guts, excitement and lantern-jawed heroes.

Here, at last, is a story that describes what it was really like. *Overlord* – the Allied code name for the D-Day landings – uses unique and authentic sources from the Imperial War Museum. Based on detailed research, incidents depicted *actually* happened. Told through one man's eyes in a straightforward but highly moving diary, *Overlord* captures as never before the feel and intensity of the war years: the brutalizing training, the boredom and sudden fear, the pathos and panic, and most of all – the terrible inadvertence of death . . .

This is the book of the award-winning film made by Stuart Cooper with screenplay by Christopher Hudson and Stuart Cooper.

Christopher Hudson has been the literary editor and chief lead writer for the *Evening Standard*, and is currently its lead book reviewer. He has written four adult books as well as the book of *The Killing Fields*. He lives in West London.

Stuart Cooper now lives in Los Angeles and has made a number of other successful films, including *A. D.* and *The Long Hot Summer*.

Overlord

CHRISTOPHER HUDSON
and
STUART COOPER

PENGUIN BOOKS

The authors would like to thank
the Imperial War Museum
and Edward R. McCosh and Finlay M. Campbell
for access to their diaries.

PENGUIN BOOKS

Published by the Penguin Group
Penguin Books Ltd, 27 Wrights Lane, London W8 5TZ, England
Penguin Books USA Inc., 375 Hudson Street, New York, New York 10014, USA
Penguin Books Australia Ltd, Ringwood, Victoria, Australia
Penguin Books Canada Ltd, 10 Alcorn Avenue, Toronto, Ontario, Canada M4V 3B2
Penguin Books (NZ) Ltd, 182–190 Wairau Road, Auckland 10, New Zealand

Penguin Books Ltd, Registered Offices: Harmondsworth, Middlesex, England

First published by Panther Books Ltd 1975
Published by Penguin Books 1992
1 3 5 7 9 10 8 6 4 2

Filmset in Monophoto Bembo

Printed in England by Clays Ltd, St Ives plc

Our pre-invasion breakfast was served at 3.00 a.m. The mess boys of the USS *Chase* wore immaculate white jackets and served hot cakes, sausages, eggs and coffee with unusual zest and politeness. But the pre-invasion stomachs were preoccupied, and most of the noble effort was left on the plates.

At 4.00 a.m. we were assembled on the open deck. The invasion barges were swinging on the cranes, ready to be lowered. Waiting for the first ray of light, the two thousand men stood in perfect silence; whatever they were thinking, it was some kind of prayer.

I too stood very quietly. I was thinking a little bit of everything: of green fields, pink clouds, grazing sheep, all the good times, and very much of getting the best pictures of the day. None of us was at all impatient, and we wouldn't have minded standing in the darkness for a very long time. But the sun had no way of knowing that this day was different from all others, and rose on its usual schedule.

June 1944
Robert Capa
Images of War

*This book is dedicated
to the cameramen and photographers
of the Second World War.*

FOREWORD

The diaries came in a pale-brown cardboard box along with a few other odds and ends: a couple of letters, some snapshots, and a gold ring in a twist of envelope marked 'Address Unknown'. There was a covering letter from Mr Philip Jackson, who lives in a suburb of Birmingham. It read as follows:

Dear Sirs,

I read in the newspaper that you were looking for material about the Second World War. Perhaps the enclosed will be of some help. I found it in the attic of my house, shortly after moving here with my wife. We have no idea who Tom Beddows is, since the previous owners of the house, who have since died, were called Jameson. Please let me know if this material is of any use to you since it is of no use to us.

The diaries are written in exercise books, in a neat painstaking hand. They tell us Tom's name, a number and rank.

One of the snapshots is a picture of Tom in uniform (inscribed on the back to Dearest Mum). It shows a young man in his early twenties, medium build, with regular features and light curly hair, looking a bit awkwardly, even uneasily, at the camera.

1941

16 APRIL

They'll be half-way home by now. Walking. Dad will have wanted to wait for a bus, and Mum will have said, 'Didn't you know there's a war on?' and they'll have set off firmly on foot down Station Road. Mum in her bunchy blue dress and lisle stockings and Dad sweating heavily in his pre-war grey suit, the one he's had as long as I can remember. They'll have taken the route that doesn't lie past the steelworks, since Dad doesn't like being reminded of work on his day off. That will take them past Mrs Crutchley, and normally they would call in for tea, since Mum will have been complaining about her feet. Except that today Mrs Crutchley is at the cemetery visiting what's left of her son after his ship went for a burton in the Atlantic. So they'll carry on home.

And I'm carrying on south to join the army. Dad told an old chum of his from the Great War. 'The poor bloody infantry,' I heard the man say. I don't know the south very well. I don't trust the people. But it's a north-country regiment, and life in an army barracks is much the same anywhere I suppose. I don't know. My thoughts are in a whirl. Ever since the call-up papers arrived, I haven't had time to sit down and think. Then it's upon you and you're away, and all the things you might have said and done are left hanging in the air. I found this empty compartment. I came in here and cried. I haven't done that for years, not since we were taken in to see Grandma and she died while she was talking to me. I don't know why I was crying. Nobody in the corridor saw

3

me because I pulled the blinds down. Was it for them? They'll be all right. Was it for me? The fact is, if I admit it, I'm quite looking forward to being in the War. Half fear and half excitement. I don't know what's going to happen but I know that something is. And nothing else is important to do until we've won or lost. It's a whole lot better than following Dad into the steelworks or catching the bus into town every day to work in a shop or a bank or as an apprentice in one of the local firms. And Mum pressing me to go to night-school in order to pass exams in chartered accountancy, so she can see me walking down the High Street in a three-piece suit. Not if I can help it.

Yes, I feel excited, and miserable too. Nothing can ever be the same again. A whole chapter of my life has closed, it's just slipped quietly away behind me like a shoreline I've left for the last time. Nobody said anything much this morning. Mum was very brave. She didn't cry, she just got very practical and bustly as if she was trying to pretend it was a day like any other. All those reminders about having everything packed and not forgetting to clean my teeth and having baths when they let me and washing my hair in case I get lice. She must think there are rats in every army barrack room. What was the last thing she said? 'Greens! Don't forget to eat a lot of greens!' That's a fine send-off.

Dad wasn't much better. That last day at work Bob★ gave me *David Copperfield* to take down to Camp. All Dad could say was, 'You won't have much time for reading. I never did.' Things have slowed up since your day, I told him. 'They're too bloody fast by half,' said Dad as I knew he would. 'Send us a letter or two and keep a diary,' he says, and, 'It won't be so bad. You'll get it out of your system there and then. It'll take your mind off things. The

---

★Tom was working on his farm when he was called up.

memories won't come back to haunt you.' He was dead serious too.

The worst thing was leaving Tina.* She was lying upstairs on the bed, and I suddenly felt so bad I had to bury my face in her and hug her tight while she licked my ear. She is so beautiful, and I shall miss her so much and the walks we had in the woods above Bob's farm, away from the noises of the city.

Somebody has come in. A soldier in uniform. A few hours from now I shall look like that.

LATER

The train hasn't started again. Most of it's still in the tunnel. We all got out on the track to watch. By that time the Messerschmitt was trying to pick up height and the Spitfire was coming in on its tail. All at once it was the Spitfire in trouble. Down here we were as quiet as mice, all of us standing on the track looking up at the sky. Even the driver had got down, you could see him along the end. You could have heard a pin drop. The next thing was that both planes circled very high into the sun. We could hear a faint buzzing, and then nothing at all; just flashes of light from the sun on the aircraft wings. Suddenly one of the planes did a dive. We couldn't see any markings, just a thin trail of black smoke that followed it down although it twisted and turned as if to leave it behind. Then a horrible thing happened. The pilot jumped out and he must have pulled his parachute cord early, just as the plane exploded. His parachute caught fire. For a moment he hung there under a ball of fire, then he dropped out of sight. What happened next was the other fighter diving down

*Tom's dog.

towards us! He was still in the sun and we all made a leap to get back into the carriages, but it was the Spitfire coming over to do a victory roll! I never felt so relieved. Some of the people stayed in the train, but I got down and waved. Hooray, we're off. About time if I'm going to get my connection in London.

SAME NIGHT

I'm lucky. There's a candle in a holder on the wall right beside me. Most of the crypt is in darkness. Some people are still trying to drown out the noise by putting cotton wool in their ears or wrapping something round their head, but most of us have stopped trying to get any sleep. Against the opposite pillar I can just make out the shape of a woman with long hair. She has been talking to her baby for five minutes now. I think she must be praying. Two men on my left are playing pocket chess by the light of the same candle. By the look of it the candle will go out before they finish their game.

We were held up for hours outside London. I woke up to find the train at a standstill and the guard carrying a gas lamp walking alongside the track, followed by a couple of railway-men in single file. It looked like something out of *A Christmas Carol*, except that they must have been looking for unexploded bombs. By the time we got in I'd missed my train to Camp.

The moon was up, quite full, but it was a cloudy night. I decided to walk south towards the river. There were a lot of bombed-out buildings, but down the Gray's Inn Road it wasn't too bad, and the old shops in High Holborn hadn't been damaged. Just as I got to Ludgate Circus the clouds cleared and the air raid warning went.

The guns started straight after that. It was like the time I visited Dad in the steel mill and stood beside the pneumatic hammer going full blow. The air vibrated and flashes lit up the sky. The noise was fantastic. I can still hear it now; a rumbling and thudding and popping of the guns, and the bombs falling and the German bombers droning up in the sky. Two fire-engines came past on their way to the City. One of the firemen shouted at me. I couldn't hear what he said. Apart from the fire-watchers on the roofs there was hardly anybody about. Three men and a woman came running down the hill to get to the shelter in Farringdon Street. One of them tripped and fell full-length on the pavement, but he got up and carried on running, clutching the back of his head with his hand. I thought of going too, but I don't think shelters are safe. Only a fortnight ago I read in the newspaper about a bomb that landed on one and killed everybody inside. Or perhaps Bob told me. I can't remember. Anyway I ran on up the hill.

That's when I fell into the hole. It wasn't very deep, and it's the luckiest thing that's ever happened to me. I fell on top of my case and didn't hurt myself except for a bruised knee, and just as I was picking myself up, a bomb went off.

Perhaps it was a parachute mine. It must have been very close. If I'd still been on the pavement it would have taken my legs off. Instead it was like someone putting tin trays against both my ears and smashing them with a hammer. I was flattened against one side of the hole and half-buried under a mound of earth and rubble. I have never been so scared. You are supposed to review all your past life, but all I could think was that I would be the one soldier who bought it before he even got to training camp. When I got out the air was thick with dust and the smell of coal gas. I had a real shock because there was a body in the middle of the road. I went over to see if it was breathing and it was a clothes dummy from a tailor's shop, which had a direct hit! I didn't wait for anything after that, but ran up the hill to the Cathedral, where some people were going in by a side door.

It was shut when I got there but I banged on it and at last a verger came and let me in. It was very eerie inside because there was a flickering red light which lit up the pews and disappeared. I turned round to ask the verger but he was already going down the stairs to the crypt. Then I saw what it was – flashes from the bombs, or perhaps a flare from the fires reflected in the stained-glass windows. I suppose it was quite a beautiful sight, but all I wanted was to get away from the bombs and hide somewhere in a dark corner. So I came down and here I am.

The man beside me has just said 'Check' quite sharply, and then apologized and said it again in a whisper. Just in time. The candle is starting to gutter. After tonight I think I know what it feels like to be in the front line.

17 APRIL

I'm glad to be out of London. Waking up in the crypt of St Paul's was like a battlefield. Bodies in sleeping-bags were strewn all around. I felt grimy and filthy from the night before. My mouth was dry and my hair was matted with dust from the explosion. It was still very dark although by my watch it was past seven o'clock and the sun should have been up. If I'd thought about it I'd have realized that after a big raid the air is as thick as a dust-cloud in summer. I had a headache and my head was still pounding with the noise of the night so at first I didn't realize that the All Clear had sounded. In fact I must have been very confused and dopey because I heard a voice coming from the altar end of the crypt and thought it was somebody telling us the way out. I picked up my case (one of the locks was hanging loose, so I knew the explosion wasn't a bad dream) and went across the crypt, stepping over the sleeping bodies. When I got close I saw three people standing round a font and a clergyman holding up a baby. It was a christening! I don't know why it was happening then and there. Perhaps the mother had come in out of the air raid last night and decided to get her baby received into the Church while it was still in the land of the living. Anyway I'd had enough of that dark place. I wanted to see London in daylight.

Many of last night's fires were still raging. I saw one whole street that seemed to be burning. As I looked the front of an office block peeled clean away and fell still burning into the middle of the road. The firemen only just got clear in time. A department store was still burning like a bonfire and flames gusted out of a third-storey window half across the street. Next door, a shop called 'Babyland' remained untouched, its windows still intact. Underfoot it was a slimy mixture of water, mud and rubble, criss-crossed with hoses and pitted with bomb craters. And hanging in the air, so stifling I could hardly breathe, was the smell of dust and plaster.

A lot of shops had been blown wide open, but I didn't see any looting. Often the shopkeepers were already at work trying to salvage what stock they could. Piling up bits of furniture or books or tins of food on the pavement, while incident officers sitting at tables totted up the local casualties. I went past the tailor's on Ludgate Hill and the man was standing stock-still on a heap of bricks and mortar. There wasn't a single thing he could lay his hands on.

Sevenoaks Station. Another half-hour to go. I'm worried about arriving at Camp late. My train was three hours late, and further delayed on the way out between Vauxhall and Clapham Junction. I tried to ring up Mum and Dad, but a lot of the lines must have been down and I couldn't get through so I wrote them a letter instead. Otherwise they'll think I copped an HE★ and will arrive back home in small parcels.

★ High explosive.

At least they won't be able to blame me for not writing, like Michael.*

That was the other thing I hadn't expected to see again. Children queuing for an evacuation train to take them to Southampton, perhaps for a ship to America. I thought most kids went off the same time Michael did last year. There they all were with their identity cards, faces pressed against the train window, some of them crying, others excited at starting a great adventure, most of them looking very serious and a little sad. Michael had been excited. I'd told him he was going to Liverpool, which he hadn't seen, and then on to Canada, which he hadn't heard of, except that Aunt Dora had sent him a postcard of a totem-pole from a place with that name. It was the one time Mum cried. Seeing him off at the station, face pressed against the glass just like those kids today. I don't know. Perhaps it was because he was helpless and didn't understand what the fuss was about. Or else she was thinking she only had two sons and the other one was old enough to go and fight. Canada's a long way off, but not so far as six foot under in a war cemetery. I hope they get my letter.

SAME NIGHT

What am I doing in this place?

18 APRIL

It's evening. I'm in the NAAFI. It's the only place I can write. I tried to write last night in bed but there wasn't time. The Barrack Room Trained Soldier is a bastard. As soon as I

*Tom's younger brother.

started, he walked up between the beds and asked in a loud voice if I was writing my history of the War. I said I wasn't, and he said, 'In that case you can turn the lights out.'

Yesterday was as bad as it could be. The train arrived in the afternoon, four hours late. The platform was deserted. I had no instructions. After a while the station-master came out on the opposite platform. He'd heard about the big raid on London over the wireless but it might as well have taken place in Wales or Outer Mongolia for all the interest he took. I told him I was for the Camp. 'The others got in last night,' he said. 'You'll have to walk. It's not many miles.' He was grinning all over his face. It was about three miles. I had to carry the case under my arm because the second lock was beginning to go. At first I thought it was a prison I was heading into. Low brick buildings with corrugated-iron roofs, a water-tower, a big, ugly stucco building which is the Company HQ, and a parade-ground the size of an airstrip on which people were being marched up one way and down the other and shouted at. It turned out to be my fault I was late, and probably my fault that Hitler had started the War in the first place. One moment I was shouted at for not calling somebody Sir, and the next I was shouted at for *calling* somebody Sir. That was the Barrack Room Trained Soldier, who isn't an officer and doesn't like to be reminded of the fact. I don't think he likes me. Yesterday when I found my barrack room, he was just lounging there on a bed reading a paperback. First he sent me out of the room for coming in without knocking and asking his permission to 'fall in', which means 'to enter', to come in the room, to open the door and make an entrance. Then he assigned me a bed and wouldn't give me time to unpack and rest. He just said, 'You're late already, haircut's next. You'll find the barber's shop next to the Company Office.' When I went out, I'm sure he ate the last of my sandwiches. Eff him. It was stale anyway.

The first thing I've learnt about the Army is that they don't

11

expect you to think. Mostly you aren't given time to think. I spent the whole of yesterday afternoon in queues. Some of them I was told to join without even knowing what they were for. First there was the queue for the barber, who was scything away in a pile of hair almost up to his knees. Then there was the queue in the army stores. We all shuffled up beside a long counter and the orderlies thrust clothes at us they thought would fit while we held out kitbags and hoped for the best. It didn't make any difference. The orderly at the end of the table gave me a cap several sizes too large and when I said something he shouted 'Next!' and pushed me out of the way. I had to lean over a table to sign for my uniform and my cap fell off in front of the Chief Store Orderly. He just said 'Next!' as if it was all he'd been trained to say.

I don't know why I fainted after the medical inspection yesterday. I don't like injections, but I've never done that before. I think it must have been everything that had happened over the last twenty-four hours. The doctor stuck the needle in me and I just keeled over. They must have thought, if he's going to do that in here, what's he going to be like in action? I felt like walking out of the Camp and going back to London to wait for a parachute mine. Anything had to be better than this. If Arthur hadn't come along, I probably would have done.

Arthur's a strange person. I like him. I'm glad he's in my barrack room. At least he's got a sense of humour. Sitting outside the MO's office afterwards I told him I didn't like injections. He said, 'Is that all? I don't like the whole sodding Army.' He said he was from East London. I started to tell him about the raid, but we were off again. More kit, more questions, more forms, the Trained Soldier making us stand by our beds while he shouted questions. Then, sleep.

Not enough sleep. This morning at roll-call I was so tired I could hardly remember my name. Breakfast was a revolting porridgy muck. Straight afterwards we had to form up and march over to the dining-room in the Company HQ to take aptitude tests. SP TEST 15 they were called. Arthur said SP stood for Silly Prick; I think he's right. It was like school again. When my pencil broke I had to put up my hand to be given another one, and after exactly twenty minutes the test was over and our pencils were taken away. I think the idea must be to sort out the people with low intelligence from the people with no intelligence at all. Write the number which when turned upside down becomes 6. That was one of the questions. Later on they got harder, we had to make a choice from alternatives: 'Map-cases are issued to officers and not to privates because 1. Privates would get the map dirty. 2. Officers usually ride in motor cars and privates don't. 3. Privates have too much equipment already. 4. Officers are less likely to lose them. 5. Privates don't have to plan actions.' After yesterday, I put down number 3. So much for my chances of becoming an officer.

20 APRIL

Who said the Sabbath shall be a day of rest? I don't think any of us like the Trained Soldier (except maybe a creep called Partridge in the end bed). It's pathetic if the man thinks he has to get us to hate him before he can teach us anything. Last night after dinner we had to have a 'dummy' kit inspection, as a dry run for the officer who normally takes the inspection on Saturday nights. We had to stand to attention by our beds while he called out our names and we answered. All our kit was laid out on the bed, and without looking at it we had to say what was there. Anything we left out was thrown across the room. He'd like to have thrown all my stuff out of the window, but I got most of it right – one pair drawers, cellular, one pair shorts PT, one forage-cap, one pair braces, one pair boots, greatcoat, socks, vests, gaiters, webbing, packs large

13

and small, battledress, gas mask, mess tins, mug, knife, fork and spoon. 'Anything else?' demanded the Trained Soldier, sticking his ugly face next to mine. I couldn't think of anything, but of course there was the pull-through, which I'd hardly heard of. So he draped it over my ears and moved on down the line to Arthur, who naturally got it all right. At the end the Trained Soldier turned round and said, 'OK, all of you, you're going to keep this lot so clean it dazzles me, and you're going to start now.' Everything has to be cleaned down to the smallest detail, from blancoing the buckle-straps on the gaiters to polishing the tops of the brasses on the webbing to blacking the laces on the boots, and if the bleeding Trained Soldier isn't satisfied, we go on until he is.

21 APRIL

It's getting a bit easier. Or maybe I'm just getting used to it. The Trained Soldier gets up first. He collects a mess tin and a spoon. Then he stands in the doorway a moment, watching us sleeping peacefully. That's the bit he really likes, because of what comes next. Banging the spoon on the back of the mess tin, he walks down the aisle between the beds, shouting at us. He always shouts the same thing – 'Up! Wash! Shave! Get dressed! Clean this barrack room and I want it shining!' We jump out of bed and do as he says. Later we stand to attention beside our beds while the Trained Soldier walks slowly past, down the aisle and back to the door. He pauses for a moment, watching us. Then he says softly, 'Breakfast.' All that for a lump of porridge.

The same kind of thing happens in the later afternoon, before dinner. It's called shining parade. We sit on our beds cleaning kit while the Trained Soldier (none of us have found out his name yet) asks us questions about the Regiment. What are the Regimental colours? How many VCs in the

Regiment? What's the name of the CSM? Of the RSM? Of the Commanding Officer? Today Arthur asked him a question instead. 'The Regiment was formed in 1685. What for? Was there any special reason?' 'What do you think?' asked the BRTS, thinking hard. 'I don't know,' said Arthur. 'To impress the bloody French!' bellowed the BRTS. He said it so loud it must have been true.

We had our first drill training this morning. Our squad NCO, a big Scotsman, addressed us on the parade-ground. It went something like this: 'Let's get two things straight right away. The first thing, the word of command "stand easy". You will not move at all until the word of command is given to you. You will not fidget, move about or anything else. Is that understood?' Then the squad shouts, 'Yes, Corporal.' Then he shouts even louder. 'Is that understood?' Then we shout even louder, 'Yes, Corporal.' It's effing insanity. We heard him the first time.

22 APRIL

Drilling all day. Nothing to write about. Or too tired to write it. The Trained Soldier came up to me this morning and said, 'Shakespeare's birthday.' Then he slunk away, laughing. I think he thinks I'm a freak.

23 APRIL

Before lights-out. Arthur has been teaching us blackjack, which a copper taught him in Stratford East. He told me that he was building up a second complete kit, which he's going to use just for inspections. All nicely polished. I'd never have thought of that.

24 APRIL

Things are getting better in this Camp. The Trained Soldier (his name's Bristow) is definitely mellowing. I've learnt a few things, like how to march and keep in step at the same time. I know the difference between a lower sling swivel and an upper sling swivel and a piling swivel, although we haven't been issued our rifles yet. And I know the entire repertoire of the NAAFI pianist. Not bad for a week.

25 APRIL

I've got to know some of the other people in my barrack room. There's Silver, a butcher's boy from Leamington Spa, who says he hates the sight of blood. I believe him. Next to me is a tall, thin, dark fellow called Young. He doesn't say much, but in civvy life he was a gardener and used to win prizes for target shooting. There's nothing he doesn't know about guns. It's all he talks about and then even Bristow gets interested enough to listen. There's Benson, a stocky character and a bit older than us other recruits. His father used to be a bookie at Newmarket. He swears so much you can't tell whether he's talking sense or not. There's Partridge, down the end, who's a creep. And next to me on the other side is Arthur, who's my best mate. He likes to think of himself as a Cockney, though Bow bells wouldn't have carried to his home even on a strong west wind.

We don't talk about the War much. We don't have to. We all know why we're here.

26 APRIL

Drilling and more drilling. Young was muttering 'Left, right, left, right' in his sleep last night. I thought he was going to get up and start sleep-marching. All our instructors use the same sentences. 'If you're told to do something you do it quickly.' 'I'll play ball with you if you'll play ball with me.' 'Remember a soldier's only as good as the equipment he's using.' I've written home and I've sent Bob a postcard to the farm.

27 APRIL

Up here it's so quiet when the planes aren't flying that I can hear the laughter of the men stringing the hop-poles four fields away. It's Sunday. The first proper time off we've had since recruit training began. I think everybody needs it. Yesterday was the hardest day so far. After morning parade we were sent off in full kit on a 'short' route march. That means ten miles cross-country, with an NCO making sure that none of us lagged behind. It was hard work. A couple of us couldn't keep up (including Vincent – nobody knows how he passed the medical). I'd have been one of them if I hadn't worked on the farm for a year. I never thought I'd be grateful to Bob for anything, it just goes to show. As soon as we got back, after washing and eating, it was time for kit inspection. The real thing this time, with Major Nickleby coming round to the barrack rooms. We were all so tired that we all left something undone, except for Arthur, who smugly brought out his second kit. Nickleby noticed everything (with me, I had neglected to blanco the belt underneath the buckle) but he still said that we were well turned out. Bristow actually smiled.

28 APRIL

We were issued our rifles today. I dropped mine by mistake.

Partridge thought that was very funny, I heard him snigger. The NCO put his mouth up to my ear and bellowed, 'That thing you just dropped is called a rifle. It is important in battle. You'll look after it more securely than any virgin. If you can't keep hold of it standing still, what the hell are you going to do with it in battle?' I didn't drop it a second time.

30 APRIL

This afternoon, bayonet training. It's the first part of the assault course they've let us use. The rest of it looks pretty frightening. We had to race across a field, climb a half-broken-down wall, and then run at these straw-filled dummies hanging from poles. One after the other. The bayonets we were given had sharp points but blunt edges. Like Arthur said, you couldn't cut a meat loaf with them, so they wouldn't be much use on Germans. But you don't use them like knives, you stick the point in, twist the bayonet and withdraw it before running on to the next one. (Always supposing you meet a German who prefers this kind of hand-to-hand combat to shooting you with his gun.)

We lined up in a row, with the dummies waiting for us on the other side of the brick wall. 'When I say Go!' said the instructor, 'you charge them, yelling as loudly as possible, like this, Aaaaarrgh!' Arthur pointed out that either the Germans would shoot us or else they'd be so frightened that they'd run away and we'd have to chase them for miles, still shouting Aaaaarrgh! It wasn't very successful the first time. Partridge tripped going over the wall and fell into a bed of nettles, which served him right. Silver ran faster than any of us, holding his bayonet out and shouting Aaaaarrgh! but he ran past all the dummies and vanished behind a shed at the end of the field. He said he'd wanted to pee, but I think it reminded him of slicing pigs back in Leamington Spa. Young lost his bayonet in one of the dummies, stopped to pull it out, and was very nearly bayoneted by Arthur coming up behind him. I stuck most of the dummies but forgot to twist the bayonet coming out, in order to spill the guts.

4 MAY

It's 5.30 and there's nobody about. It's quite eerie. I've never seen the Camp so deserted. Even Vincent's stopped nursing his cough in the barrack room and gone out somewhere. Most people have gone to the cricket match on the village green. Camp against Village. Arthur's supposed to be behind the score-board, but he'll go off to the boozer in half an hour when it opens and the game will collapse. Silver and Partridge borrowed a couple of bikes to go up and see the ruins. They won't be back until roll-call. Nor will Benson. He's got a date with the girl who makes deliveries in her brother's van.

If it hadn't been for yesterday I'd be at the cricket match now instead of confined to barracks. It was a bleeding silly thing to do. Like Arthur said, I could have killed myself. But by the time I thought about it I was on the way down. It was partly his fault, not that it matters. Being a route march, as opposed to a 'short' route march, the Lieutenant-Corporal wasn't keeping such a close check on us. It also meant fifteen miles, in the hot sun. We'd been climbing a really steep hill, bending right forward to make our packs help push us forwards. Arthur had been grumbling and going slower and slower. He said he was tired but the real reason was that he wanted a fag. So we stopped at the top, when the NCO and the others had already started a slow descent and weren't likely to come back looking for us. Arthur was less chirpy than usual. I asked him what the matter was and he brooded about it, taking long drags at the cigarette. Then he told me about his girl back in London. It seems he was engaged to her

19

(betrothed, he said, which made it sound more serious) and they'd planned to get married. Then Arthur was called up and her Dad refused to let them marry until the War was over. 'Wait until after we've won the War,' was the way he put it. Arthur said he was a right bugger, and he'd let the Jerries poke his wife if they so much as knocked at the door.

Anyway, we got talking about other things. Arthur said he'd wanted to fly but he'd failed the medical. They found that he was slightly colour-blind. I told him about the dogfight above the train on the way to London, how we'd all scrambled back into the carriages when it was just the RAF pilot doing a victory roll. While we were talking a couple of fighters flew low over the ridge of hills, banked and dipped over the horizon. Arthur reckoned they were prototypes to replace the Hurricane. Maybe he's right. He's pretty sharp about most things, he even looks like a weasel, with carroty hair, very neat and compact. After the War he's going to buy a garage and set up a scrap-metal business on the side. He's going to buy obsolete war machinery, keep it a few years while its scrap value appreciates, and then make a killing. He invited me to go in with him, but I said no. I don't know why, it's a good idea. It's not as if there's anything else I want to do. But something stops me thinking that far ahead.

I don't know how long we were talking. We lost track of the time, that was the stupid thing. When we got up and went to the edge, there were the others directly below us. They'd taken the path down and were a good ten minutes ahead. I thought we ought to go straight down, over the edge. Arthur said I was mad. I suppose he was right, but it didn't look too steep from where I was standing, just a grassy slope through some bushes which dipped out of sight. I started down. Arthur tried to stop me. I had a feeling, I remember this, that I had nothing to lose. Nothing to lose. Even when the ground got steeper and fell away and I couldn't stop and went head over heels, with a giddy sensation, falling and

20

bumping on rocks and stones, going faster and faster until I hit my head on something hard and blacked out. When I came round, I was sitting propped up against a tree. The others were around me and the Corporal was dabbing my head with a cloth. They'd watched the whole thing, thinking they were going to have to take a corpse back to Camp. But apparently my pack snagged against a rock and broke my fall. I bounced the rest of the way, losing nothing worse than my helmet and rifle.

I think the charges that landed me in the guardroom were endangering my equipment and my life, in that order, and failing to carry out a route march in proper order. Arthur could have been nabbed on that last one too. But, typical, the delay while the Corporal decided what to do with me was long enough for him to slink into the section without anybody noticing. I was taken back to Camp. The MO gave me iodine and a plaster. I was taken to the guardroom. The guardroom orderly stuffed the magazine he was reading into a desk drawer and wrote my particulars into a large register. Then I was marched down an antiseptic-smelling corridor and left-turned into a cell. The door was shut and locked. I took my boots off, lay down, and fell asleep. It felt like the safest place in Britain.

I think they must have been lenient with me. So Bristow was saying this morning. They only kept me in there one night. When they threw my kitbag in, the orderly hadn't bothered to take my safety razor out, which is something they normally do. About ten o'clock I was woken up by the noise of a drunk being hauled down the corridor into the cell opposite. At least, he sounded half-seas-over. But how anyone could get even mildly sloshed on the watery beer they serve in the NAAFI I can't imagine.

The cell was quite bare apart from the mattress, blankets and a small sink and bucket. I suppose I should have felt depressed or remorseful, but I wasn't either. Instead I felt free, quite free, in this prison within a prison. There was nowhere I wanted to be, nobody I wanted to see, nothing I wanted to do. I could have stayed in that cell for days. Lost in the heart of the machine, with only a ventilator shaft to connect me with the outside world. It was a new feeling, this sense that I have nothing to lose, no matter what happens. It put me at peace with myself. I don't know where it came from, but it helped me, and it's still with me now.

I was woken by 'Love divine, all loves excelling' coming through the ventilator shaft. Once a month the Chaplain holds an early-morning service before Communion, and this was it. I was told to wash and dress and was marched out to the guardroom office, where I was officially discharged with the caution that I had to stay within the limits of the Camp all today. So here I am, sitting in a patch of grass outside the barrack room, edging away from the afternoon shadows. Vincent's back, and gone to the NAAFI for a lemonade. I bet Arthur's gone for a booze-up and left the cricketers to keep score.

5 MAY

Letter from Bob. His aunt and uncle both killed outright after a direct hit on their home in Middlesex.

8 MAY

I've got used to writing in the NAAFI now. I don't mind the noise, it's finding a bit of table that isn't sticky with spilt beer or canned peach juice.

After morning parade we had another session of assault-course training. Not the bayonets, this time – much tougher than that. We lined up in full kit, carrying rifles, in front of a ramp that led down into an artificial lake about thirty yards wide and a hundred yards long. At the far end was a vertical wall thirty feet high with three rope-ladders hanging down into the water. The NCO stood at the top of the wall with a Very pistol to start us. It made me think of school sports day. No other instructor uses a Very pistol. He could just as easily have raised a flag, but he had found it in the stores and it made him feel important.

He fired the pistol and we ran into the lake shouting loudly, not to frighten the enemy but because the water was cold. It was quite deep too, and Arthur had to hold back and help Vincent, who can't swim and was frightened of the water going over his head. I was quite scared myself, because the kit dragged us down and we had to keep our rifles dry by holding them over our heads. It was hard to get hold of the rope-ladder. I had to grab it with one hand and haul myself up high enough to sling my rifle on my shoulder and get a second hand free to go on climbing. On the next ladder, Benson, who'd tried to climb one-handed, slipped and fell back into the water, nearly knocking out Partridge, who was climbing below him. And all this time the NCO was screaming at us from the top and Vincent was yelling down below as Arthur tried to fix him on the rope-ladder. Once we were all up the wall we weren't given time to dry out or anything. The NCO led us off at a jogtrot down through some woods to a deep stream. I thought we were going to have to wade through that too, but instead the NCO took us along the bank and showed us how we were going to have to cross it – on two wires above the stream, while mines go off in the water below.

The last stage today was running at full tilt along a narrow woodland track, rifle at the ready, dodging large punch-bags that were swung at us from either side and at the same time looking at the path ahead to try and avoid camouflaged pits that we might fall into. The whole thing was weird. It reminded me of the Ghost Tunnel at the Spring Fair, where as schoolboys we travelled around on a rickety train screeching with laughter while skeletons in luminous green wobbled close by. Arthur thought this part of the course must have been dreamed up by big white hunters used to trapping elephants and savages in darkest Africa. He said he'd given up trying to explain to the NCO that any future British Expeditionary Force wasn't likely to be met by jackbooted Nazis behind trees swinging punch-bags at us, although he did ask why we hadn't been issued with blowpipes!

9 MAY

The Company Commander made a short speech after he'd inspected kit this evening: ten more days of basic training, then on to join our units for 'anti-invasion exercises'. This is depressing if it's true. Most of the British Army seems to have been doing anti-invasion exercises since Dunkirk. From the sound of it they're turning into a sort of glorified Home Guard, doing manoeuvres and patrols against an imaginary enemy which can't get across the Channel. There was a rumour that my Regiment was being sent out to reinforce British troops in Greece. I don't see why not. After all, we've been fighting out there for a month now and don't seem to have made much headway. Young must have been thinking the same thing as me. When the Commander finished, he said, 'Permission to speak, sir. What about Greece, sir?' Nickleby just said, 'What about Greece?' and went out of the door.

10 MAY

Young's just got his marksman's badge, so if the Krauts do invade, I suppose he'll be made a sniper. After the rest of the

Regiment has begun retreating north towards the Isle of Sheppey, Young will be left to defend Margate from the upper window of a Ladies' Boarding House. Not that anyone here takes the idea of invasion very seriously any more. The most serious subject tonight is Benson's girlfriend, who we call the delivery girl. She didn't deliver today. Instead she sent a note to him saying she was pregnant and either he must marry her or she'd go to see his commanding officer. Benson is terrified. For one thing, he has a wife in Cambridge. For another, the girl's brother is coming back from leave next week. For another, he doesn't know what the CO would do. Partridge thought it would be a court-martial. Arthur said that a hundred years ago they'd let adulterers off with one hundred lashes but the punishment had got more severe since then. But Benson has just worked out that she can't be more than 'four days late'. Four days late doing what he didn't say, but he sounded very relieved. The real surprise was Vincent's girlfriend. He passed round a photograph of her this evening — a real stunner with long dark ringlets and a lovely smile. Benson asked if it wasn't his sister because they looked so alike. I think he's envious, because the delivery girl is plain-looking and has fat thighs. Vincent has turned out to be really nice. Although he's awake coughing half the night and seems continually tired-out, he never complains or goes to cadge sick-leave off the MO. He keeps up very pluckily with the rest of us.

11 MAY

The first reports are just coming in.

Nothing is very clear yet, but it sounds as if London has had its biggest air raid yet. Bigger than the one I got caught in on the way down. I knew something was happening because I heard the drone of the bombers all night flying overhead. Hundreds of them. About two o'clock in the morning I heard a bomb in the distance. Just a faint 'crump', but the windows shook all the same. It may have been one of the Heinkels, driven off by flak and having to jettison its bombs on the homeward flight path. According to the bulletin I heard, the water pressure was low and the firemen couldn't cope with some of the worst fires until early this morning. The strange thing is that it was a full moon last night, the worst weather for bombing. It seems that Air Command was able to send up day-fighters and we knocked out a good number of German bombers. Everybody here thinks it's some sort of victory. Having been in an air raid three and a half weeks ago (it seems years ago) I know different.

SAME NIGHT

I've just told Arthur and he thinks it's very funny. I don't know why. It was his idea we should go in the first place. We were given the afternoon off, and we decided to borrow bicycles and ride into town to see the new Clark Gable film at the Picture Palace. I bought my ticket and went in, leaving Arthur to talk to a couple of girls who'd been hanging around outside. It was the last I saw of him. Inside it was dark, and nearly empty since it was the matinée. I was in time to see Movietone News, which was weeks old as usual and still showing 'our brave lads' fighting brilliantly victorious battles in Greece in the teeth of German aggression. I wish I was out there. Even a film cameraman gets closer to the action. After that came *The Way To His Heart*, a comic short film in silent-movie style with captions encouraging viewers to eat more spuds. It said there are a hundred and one ways of using them!

Just as the main film was starting, this woman came and sat next to me. As most of the cinema was empty it seemed a strange thing to do, although all I noticed at first was the strong perfume she was wearing. About the time Clark Gable meets the Girl and it was getting very moving and romantic, this woman put her hand on my leg and said, 'Do you have a light, honey?' I don't know who she thought I was, an American or something. I said, 'A light?' and she said, 'That's right, soldier, a light.' So I got out a box of matches and lit one. All this time Gable is talking to the Girl and leading her out on to the balcony in the moonlight. She leaned right over me, blocking out the picture and guiding my hand towards her cigarette, which I always hate. She was very brightly made up, as far as I could see in the flame, with heavy lipstick and eye-shadow. Probably a shop-girl with the day off, although she looked a bit old for that. I didn't really notice, because I was trying to hear what Clark Gable was saying. He'd sat down with the Girl at a table overlooking an ornamental lake and was leaning across, speaking in a low voice and touching her fingers. Meanwhile this woman wanted to know if I was on leave. I said I wasn't, so she asked if I was a deserter, which seemed a bit much. Then the Girl looked at Clark Gable with misty eyes and said, 'Want a bit of fun?', or I thought it came from the Girl, but it was this woman in the next seat! I didn't know what to say. So she asked me again in a louder voice, 'Want a bit of fun?' I said I would prefer to be left alone, looking round to see if anyone had heard or if Arthur had come in, which he hadn't. 'Come on, darling,' said this dreadful woman. Beside the ornamental lake the music had started on the violins. I felt a prickling sensation on my leg and looked down to see her fingers with long red finger-nails marching up towards the top of it. Heaven knows what she thought she was doing. I got up and walked out of the cinema without looking back. Outside I found my bicycle had been stolen. I asked the woman at the box-office and she said the soldier who'd been talking to the girls had put one of them on my bicycle and ridden off with her. So I walked back to Camp. If Arthur thinks that's funny he's a slob.

Went out to the pub tonight with Silver. Only four more days to go. Silver is a nice, steady bloke. He's the sort of soldier who got killed in their millions in the trenches during the First War. In fact he's exactly the type the Army like. If he is told to do something he does it dependably well – it wouldn't occur to him to do it differently from how he'd been told, or to do anything else. He might not have many brains, but he's not foolish and he's got a lot of courage. Tonight he said something which surprised me. He said he very nearly applied to be a conscientious objector, a pacifist. He didn't want to kill anybody and didn't see why anyone else should. He hated the first few days of recruit training. Then, he said, he saw it had nothing to do with killing people at all. He thought we were going to be trained killers. Instead it's marching up and down hills, turning left and right on a parade-ground, sticking knives in straw sacks and learning how to take a rifle apart and put it together again. It is much less bloodthirsty than chopping pigs and you aren't as liable to cut yourself. I nearly asked him if he thought that was how it was going to be when we go into battle. I didn't, because I know Silver can't think ahead that far. He's one of the lucky ones.

Perhaps I've got too much imagination. I'm given plenty to feed it on. I got talking to a man of about forty in civvy clothes. He was drinking hard and his hand shook when he picked up the beer mug. He was an off-duty fireman, the brother of the landlord, who worked in London and had come down 'to get away for a few days'. He had been on duty south of the river on the night of 10–11 May, the night of the big raid. He didn't want to speak about it at first. Then I mentioned being in London during the earlier raid, and he opened up. 'Either people have been through it, or you'll never get them to understand,' he said.

It was worse than anything he'd seen. The incendiaries started plummeting down at eleven o'clock, and the first calls were picked up at the station a few minutes later. He lost count of how many fires he attended that night. He was still working at seven in the morning. He said he'd thought they'd never finish putting them out and London would burn until there was nothing left. He was working with firemen from as far away as Bristol and Birmingham and still there weren't nearly enough fire appliances to cope. Not enough pumps, not enough water. One place that had gone up quite early was a tea warehouse. The chests broke open, the water from their hoses boiled in the enormous heat and the street was soon awash with well-brewed Ceylonese tea. At least nobody was killed in that one. In the next 'incident', as they're called, an incendiary had fallen into a terraced house in Southwark. Normally they wouldn't have covered it, since public buildings and military installations had priority and that night there wasn't much time for anything else. It just happened that the house was next to a depot for Guy's Hospital. The house was ablaze, and a woman was trapped on the second floor. They got a ladder up to the window just as smoke began to pour through. The woman was holding a young child and leaning out of the window with it. As the fire burst in the woman leant out further. The child started to struggle. He went up that ladder faster than he'd ever done before. As he leaned across to the window, the child struggled free and dropped. The woman screamed and ran back into the house, into the fire. He tried to follow her but was driven back by the heat. 'She must have wanted to get that kid,' he said. 'The whole house was blazing but she got nearly to the bottom of the stairs.'

He talked about other 'incidents' too. About people alive one moment, yelling and waving, and the next, bodies exploding in the heat like paper bags. Twice that night he'd had someone die in his arms. He'd been a fireman all his life, but said he wouldn't be able to cope with another night like that. I left the pub and walked back by myself. It is very green and soft, this part of England. There is something deceptive about it, or unreal. Fifty miles south is enemy-occupied France. Fifty miles north is London. I am between two wars, and a part of neither.

16 MAY

Vincent was killed today.

17 MAY

There is going to be a special service tomorrow. His mother and father have been notified. Notified. Nobody has told Vincent's girlfriend because there was no address on the back of the photograph.

Vincent's death is accounted for in the following letter home, postmarked 17 May:

'Dear Mum and Dad,

. . . It happened on the assault course, the final one, the one the Sergent called 'Commando-style'. We had to cover the whole of it yesterday, including crossing the river on wires and crawling under the bridge with the river running high. At the end of it we had to attack a ruined farmhouse from which the enemy would be firing blanks, using what cover we could and ferreting them out with smoke-bombs. Three squads took part, making up a full platoon. The first five into the farmhouse were to be given some sort of award by the CO.

Of course it was raining. It was bound to be. Coming down really hard, too. Nobody thought much of it since we were going to get wet anyway. The thirty of us fitted on our bayonets and at a signal from the Sergeant raced across the field, climbed the wall and jabbed at the dummies, swearing and shouting all the while. Then we crawled through a brambly hedge and slid down the ramp into the swimming-pool, as it's become known. It was easier this time. I flicked the rifle on to my shoulder (nearly cutting my throat on the bayonet which I'd forgotten about) and shinned up the rope-ladder. At the top of the wall I looked back. Vincent was still in the water struggling towards the rope-ladder. Arthur was holding on to the ladder and reaching out towards him. It was the last I saw of him.

I ran on towards the stream, just behind Silver, who was shaking the water off him like a dog. The bank path was barred. We had to climb a tree overhanging the stream and walk across it on the wire like a trapeze artist, clutching another wire at head level to keep our balance. Then along the opposite bank until a barrier forced us into the stream and under a tiny bridge, more like a large pipe, one man at a time, keeping our heads above water. The rain had already raised the water level to the point that made this impossible without holding your breath and going under. It was very nasty.

Out then along Arthur's wild game path, ahead of Silver (who'd been knocked off the trapeze wire by an explosion in the stream) and a few yards behind Benson, who is very fit. However, he suddenly disappeared down a hole and I ran on, ducking the punch-bags, into open country. There was another hedge to crawl through, a plank ladder over barbed wire, and then the farmhouse right ahead. I started ducking and trying to use cover, as I'd seen Indian trackers do in Westerns, but then Silver ran right past me,

31

disdaining enemy blanks, and threw a smoke-bomb into the farmhouse. So I stood up and followed him in and we captured two annoyed lance-corporals, who were convinced that we should have fallen, riddled with bullets, several hundred yards away.

We bribed them to silence with a half-share in our award from the CO and together we waited for the others to arrive. Within minutes they were all there, chucking their smoke-bombs around, all except Vincent and another man called Daniels. We waited for a quarter of an hour with the two NCOs and eventually Daniels appeared, holding up his trousers, which he'd ripped to shreds falling on the barbed wire. By this time the Sergeant was with us. He organized a search party to go back and look for Vincent. Arthur and I volunteered for it. Arthur said he'd helped Vincent up the rope-ladder, so we knew he couldn't be that far back. Most likely he'd fallen into a pit on the wild game path and couldn't get out. We retraced the ground, over the barbed wire, through the hedge and down the punch-bag trail. There was no sign of Vincent. Then we came to the stream. It was unrecognizable. The heavy rain had released some barrier upstream and turned it into a muddy torrent flowing fast under the bridge and flooding on to the banks either side. Lodged under the branches of a tree was Vincent's body. His face looked up at us from under water. His mouth was open like a fish. His left foot had entangled in the tree and it took three or four minutes to pull him out.

Daniels was the last person to see him alive. He heard a cry and turned at the bridge to see Vincent fall off the wires into the stream, which was already flowing more fiercely than when Silver and I had passed. Daniels went under the bridge holding his breath to get to the other side. Before running on, he looked round and saw that Vincent had somehow got to the bank and hauled himself up and onwards to the bridge. Ducking under the bridge, his heavy pack already sodden with water, he would have fought his fear of drowning all the way. But he couldn't hold his breath any longer.

Tom

A photograph of Vincent was found with Tom's letter. Inscribed on the back in tiny handwriting was the following Wilfred Owen poem:

> *Move him into the sun —*
> *Gently its touch awoke him once,*
> *At home, whispering of fields unsown.*
> *Always it woke him, even in France,*
> *Until this morning and this snow.*
> *If anything might rouse him now*
> *The kind old sun will know.*
>
> *Think how it wakes the seeds,*
> *Woke, once, the clays of a cold star.*
> *Are limbs, so dear-achieved, are sides,*
> *Full-nerved — still warm — too hard to stir?*
> *Was it for this the clay grew tall?*
> *— O what made fatuous sunbeams toil*
> *To break earth's sleep at all?*

It may be of interest that on 17 May Tom was eighteen years old.

18 MAY

Last full day of training camp. Tomorrow we'll be taken to our units.

This morning all the recruits lined up on the parade-ground by platoon for inspection by top brass. We stood there shining and still, like tin soldiers, while he got out of his car and strolled up and down the ranks, poking at us with his swagger-stick and talking to the CO about the weather. Our uniforms were spotlessly clean. Much cleaner than Vincent's when we pulled him out of the water. Not that the top brass would have been told about that. It would have spoiled the grand occasion.

After all, who was Vincent? For most people in this Camp he was a name, to be crossed off registers and erased from lists on the notice-board. Nobody is much involved. The CO has to write a letter to his parents. The store orderlies have to repossess his kit and hand it out to the next recruit. The laundry detail have to take the sheets and blankets off his bed and turn the mattress. The BRTS has to see that his few possessions are parcelled up and sent home.

And the Chaplain has to take a funeral service. I went to it, along with the rest of our barracks. It didn't take long. The Chaplain read the lesson from St Paul: 'The last enemy that shall be destroyed is death. Death is swallowed up in victory.' I looked at Arthur, who was crying. It's all very well for us. If we die in action it might well be on the way to victory. It might be in the moment of victory. There won't be time for a funeral service and there won't be any need for one. But Vincent's death seems so futile. It hasn't anything to do with victory. It isn't so easy to swallow.

The next entry is not dated. We think it was written some time in June. Tom appears to have stopped making regular entries after Vincent's death or after he was posted to his unit.

I'm writing this near the Castle. It's a long way even by bicycle, but it was worth the journey. The Castle ruins stand by themselves in the middle of a green valley, very quiet and enclosed. Hidden by trees on the far side of a small stream is an old stone church. High up on the slope overlooking the ruins is a great grey Gothic mansion. Otherwise there is nothing for miles around. The ruins produce a feeling of restfulness as if they have survived the worst that will happen to them and it hasn't destroyed their reason for being here. Already I'm feeling easier about the nightmare I had last night.

For some reason I'd met Mum and Dad in town and left them to see a film while I walked back to my old Camp with Tina. Camp was strangely deserted. I heard the bombers in the distance but I was paralysed with fear and couldn't run to take cover. Bombs started falling all around me. Tina slipped her lead and ran off. As I followed her, the single-storey barracks suddenly reared up to three or four storeys and started spouting fire. Tina ran into one of the burning buildings. I followed her up the stairs. The paint on the walls was bubbling. The stairs fell away behind me. Tina yelped and screamed, her coat was burning. She jumped out on to a ledge and barked for me to come to her rescue. I got to the window and leaned out, but the whole building seemed to be falling and the next moment I was on my knees in a wood, crawling out of a puddle. I was by myself. Bombs were still falling and there was cross-fire from machine-guns. I ran as hard as I could, splashing through puddles, while bullets flicked past me and buried into trees on either side. Suddenly I came to the edge of the wood. The guns stopped. In the silence I could distinctly hear the call of a song-thrush. The wind stopped. Nothing moved, but I was still running. Then a voice screamed: 'Get down there! Get down!' There was an enormous explosion and a body was flung through the air (or I was flung towards the body, I'm not sure). I went up to it with a sickening feeling, knowing who it would be, knowing I would have to turn it over and make sure. His body was quite dry, dressed in a German uniform. In his wallet was a postcard, a prescription, a lock of hair from his girlfriend and a photograph of himself in uniform, looking at the camera with an uneasy smile. As I held it up to study it, it was taken out of my hand and put on a mantelpiece next to a black-edged card. It was our mantelpiece at home and it had become a photograph of me. That's when I woke up.

LATER

It's very serene here. I've just been woken by the sound of an approaching Wellington. It's evening, I've been asleep for hours. The Wellington passed so low over the Castle I thought it might crash – its droning engines invading the valley. What a magnificent, devastating sight. The afterglow of the day's light glinting off its wings. Sudden reflections off the Perspex nose. I thought for a moment I could see the gunner moving around. If you were deaf you would think the plane was drifting, gliding, sliding up, instead of being pulled by power-ful engines out over the Channel towards its target. My God, what towns will burn tonight?

The following clipping from The Times, *dated Saturday 14 June 1941, reporting a raid on the Ruhr, was found loose in the back of the Diary.*

Germany's industrial centre, the Ruhr, experienced its heaviest raid of the War on Thursday night, when a very powerful force of RAF Bomber Command aircraft attacked it in waves from midnight until an hour or so before dawn.

Throughout the length and breadth of this vital area of fifty miles the British machines left a patchwork of fires which showed up gutted warehouses and allowed our crews to watch huge pieces of buildings hurled into the air by some of the heaviest bombs. In spite of the adverse weather the raid was a complete success. Thick cloud and ground haze in the valley did not prevent many of the pilots from diving low to release their flares and then their bombs. Incendiary bombs also lighted the path. The bomber force employed was so strong that at no time throughout the night were there fewer than three aircraft over any target at the same time. In addition to putting up a heavy anti-aircraft barrage, the Germans were employing a number of night fighters and there were a number of indecisive combats. In one, however, a German fighter was almost certainly destroyed.

The Air Ministry announcement issued yesterday said: 'On Thursday night a very large force of aircraft of Bomber Command carried out a successful attack on industrial targets in the Ruhr. The attack was the heaviest carried out in a single night against this industrial area and a great weight of bombs was dropped. Many industrial buildings were destroyed by high-explosive bombs and a large number of fires were started. Six aircraft of Bomber Command are missing. Aircraft of Coastal Command on Thursday night attacked the docks at Brest and Antwerp and targets near Rotterdam. One aircraft of Coastal Command is missing from these operations.'

21 AUGUST

Today was Dad's birthday. I was thinking about that when I had the accident. Forty-three years old. He looks about seventy, with his white hair, and I know why. When he was my age he was fighting the Germans face to face, not looking at them through binoculars like me. Six feet down in a muddy dug-out, with the smell of rotting bodies which never lifts no matter how much lime is sprinkled. He wrote to me about it the other day. I'd been complaining and he said he wrote to prove that us home-based lot are living the life of Riley. But I think that's an excuse for getting things off his chest.

The example he gave was of an attack his company had made across a few hundred yards of craters and stricken trees that were all that was left of a beech wood. A number of men went missing, including his best friend, but the attack was a success and they occupied some of the German trenches. Fighting was fierce, with the Germans entrenched only yards away. There was no time to get the corpses out. He had to crouch on top of them or stick them into the sides of the trench with a bayonet. Then the Jerries counter-attacked and Dad got out just in time. It was a pitch-black night and they were retreating through the beech wood, a fortnight after they'd secured it behind the front line. Dad took cover in what he thought was a shell-hole. It turned out to be a drainage ditch, with rats that scuttled away from a dark shape beside him.

When daylight came, Dad found he'd been sharing the ditch with his best friend. Dad knew him from his wrist-watch since the rest had been eaten away. He took the watch and had it mailed to the man's widow together with a letter of sympathy. He said her husband had been afforded a decent burial. What else could he say?

Forty-three and an old man. He'd have aged even quicker if I'd copped it this afternoon. Riding back towards the barracks down a narrow stretch of road, an army lorry turned the corner at speed and roared towards me, taking up the whole road. I swerved the bicycle into a ditch, pitched off the saddle and hit my head on a fence post. It must have stunned me for a moment because I don't remember the lorry not stopping. Instead there was a woman beside me, patting my hand anxiously and asking me if I was all right. She was about thirty, I suppose, attractive and rather sad-looking, with high cheek-bones and nice wrinkles round her eyes. I picked myself up and tried to get back on my bike, but wobbled and nearly fell off, so she suggested I should come into her cottage opposite for a cup of tea.

The cottage was very comfortable and cosy. She'd just

made some flapjacks to go with the tea, so it was quite a set-up. I called her Ma'am, but she said her name was Mrs Galloway. She seemed very interested in the Army, wanting to know my regiment and so forth. 'It must be terribly hard,' she said, 'to know that you might be called up at any time to die for your country.' I couldn't think of any answer to this, except to tell her what Dad had said, that it was hardest of all for the ones left behind.

Mrs Galloway went pale when I said this. I could have cut my tongue out. I'd noticed the photograph of an airman on the mantelpiece, but I hadn't connected her with being a widow. I began to say I was sorry, but she cut in. 'In a war, everybody suffers,' she said. Her husband had been a bomber pilot. Coming back from a mission over Germany his plane had been caught by flak. Although badly wounded, he kept the plane on course and didn't order the navigator to bale out until they were over the English coast. His navigator baled out without realizing that Galloway couldn't move from the cockpit. The plane crash-landed and Galloway was killed.

It was obvious from the way his widow talked that they had been very much in love. They'd only been married a short time. She had sold their house and moved up to this remote cottage to be alone for a while. She was very passionate in a way, but also very dignified and self-possessed. She was learning to live with herself. She showed me some of his things. 'The only thing you can do with memories like that is to let them grow familiar, so they can't take you horribly by surprise,' she said. There were letters, of course, tied up with white ribbon. A silver cigarette case – 'He always carried it in his breast pocket, since he'd read of one deflecting a fatal bullet.' A broken lighter. A few photographs – one showing Galloway with some of his squadron, another with his wife beside a beautiful lake ('in Italy on our honeymoon,' said his widow). A pocket-book, stained and crumpled. A fountain-pen. Four lucky coins and a little woolly bear mascot which Mrs Galloway had given him to wear round his neck.

It was half-way between a museum and a shrine, with her as caretaker and congregation. There must be hundreds of these little museums already up and down the country. Today she wanted to share her grief. I wanted to comfort her but I couldn't. For that afternoon I was half-way between husband and son to her. She wanted me as a witness. She bathed the bump on my head with cold water, and didn't object when I said I had to go. I want to go back there and see her. But it would make no difference. Her husband protects her in death as he cared for her in life. She is a part of his death. I see what Dad meant now, and how terrible war can be to people who never hear a shot fired in anger. For them the war never stops, and death which comes to us once is for them repeated over and over again.

26 DECEMBER

Stayed with Arthur's people in Walthamstow over Christmas. First time in London since April. With no air raids for the last month, it's a different city. Arthur's dad says that 6,000 civilians were killed and as many injured in April, most of them in London. I'm lucky I wasn't one of them. Blitz habits remain, though. Arthur's people got in a half-size Christmas tree, so that if the sirens went, it could be taken down to the basement with them.

His sister was there with her children, both very young. It made me realize that I hadn't had a chance to be with children since Michael went off to Canada. Christmas for them is as good and exciting as it's always been. As a special treat, on Boxing Day, they were taken into the country to collect holly. The little girl is the bossy one. She made her brother lie flat on his back for minutes on end, while she put on a white coat and pretended to be a nurse in the ATS.

Arthur found some mistletoe, of course, and kissed his

girlfriend under it for so long that his dad had to tap him on the shoulder and ask if other people could have a go. We sang carols, ate a nice piece of chicken, and listened in the evening to a Sherlock Holmes detective story done on the wireless.

This afternoon, depressed by the news about Hong Kong,★ went to see Clark Gable in *Honky Tonk* at the Empire. Lana Turner is smashing. Cup of tea, then caught the train from Fenchurch Street back to my unit.

This is the last entry in Tom's first diary. Three other exercise books were in the cardboard box. One of these, for 1942, had been waterlogged at some time and so badly damaged as to be virtually unreadable. The other two exercise books take up the story at the beginning of 1944, when Tom was on his way to a battle school for D-Day assault training.

Tom's 1943 diary was not in the box. We contacted Mr Philip Jackson, who had found the diaries and who had written the covering letter. He replied that he had made a search for additional material and had come up with no other records of Tom or his family.

We had already written to the address on the envelopes of Tom's letters to his mother and father and received no reply. We therefore got in touch with local government offices in Sheffield to discover from council records what had happened to the family. We learnt that the address no longer existed. The house had been pulled down several years ago, and the ground cleared for a new housing development. We also established, with the help of Sheffield records, that Mr and Mrs Beddows moved from the area as long ago as 1946. No forwarding address remained.

From the damaged 1942 diary, little can be pieced together. Two fragments mentioning St Nazaire suggest that Tom may have taken part in the combined Army, Navy and Air Force raid on the night of 27 March. But Tom never once refers to the St Nazaire operation

★ Hong Kong surrendered after a seventeen-day siege.

41

in the 1944 diaries. The phrase 'special duties' recurs on two consecutive pages, together with references to Scotland, which lead us to suppose that Tom spent some time in the north, possibly with a VIP guard detachment, or else on commando training. Nothing further can be deduced.

1944

28 JANUARY

Eighteen months we've been waiting for this. Rumours. counter-rumours, and suddenly we're told to pack up and get ready to move at twenty-four hours' notice. Destination, a 'battle school' somewhere down on the South Coast. As vague as that. It's typical of the Army to do things this way. You think the powers that be have forgotten you, sending you to obscure parts of East Anglia on anti-invasion exercises to impress the locals. You bask in obscurity while other units fight for acres of sand in Tunisia or charge up the Italian peninsula liberating sexy signorinas. All at once the lighthouse beam swings round and focuses you in its glare. The easy life is over. Picture-palaces, paperbacks, parachute patrols become a thing of the past. Everything is urgent and vitally important. One moment we're in our barracks with the months stretching ahead. The next it's quick march to the railway station and we're stopping and starting, shunting and sidling, half-way across Britain with only a mug of lukewarm tea and a cheese sandwich slightly curled at the edges between us and starvation. At least we've started. And what a relief! I can't think of anything else. It's like that first time I left home all those months ago. A mixture of fear and excitement.

Thinking about that first journey, I can't help noticing the differences. The women for one thing. We went past the engine yard at Didcot and it was like an Amazon take-over. There were women porters, women signalmen, a woman station-master and women in overalls cleaning out the engines!

This morning, coming further south, there were military vehicles everywhere. Many of them were American. Private cars were heavily outnumbered. We went past woods and areas of common land which had been cordoned off with notices reading 'Army Property – Keep Out'. They were about the only notices around. Most of the signposts and place-names in this part of the world seem to have disappeared altogether. I suppose it all adds up to one big difference. On that first journey the War seemed like a kind of alien pattern imposed on the landscape. Sombre and threatening like a storm-cloud blotting out the common light of day. Now the whole country is geared up for battle. The War seems natural to it. I don't just mean we're in a state of readiness. It's more than that. By now everybody has had to adapt themselves. Everything, big or little, has had to make adjustments to the War. The whole place has shifted on its axis to concentrate on striking back.

It can't be long now – so Jack seems to think, and he's the sort of person you can believe in. We talked most of yesterday and I feel I've known him as long as Arthur or Bob Young. It's funny to think I only met him the day before, when they merged our two units prior to departure. His lot tend to keep to themselves. It must be very hard for someone like Jack. He volunteered in 1939, so he's already had four and a half years of it and wishes to God the whole damned thing was over. The new movement orders don't impress him at all. Like he says, you spill your blood and guts to help the Belgians and then four years later you get ready to spill them again to help the bloody French. And in between, here he is going paddling down on the South Coast, learning how to keep his bloody rifle dry. Jack's view of the War is a simple one. It varies, depending on his mood, from the MMU to the IMMU (Military Muck-Up and Imperial Military Muck-Up). At the moment it's mostly IMMU. He's been in His Majesty's Forces since the outbreak of hostilities (nice phrase). He's seen active service in North Africa and he doesn't like the idea of going back to battle school one bit.

I was talking to him about it half an hour ago. He came in here with a couple of apples he's filched off the GIs up the corridor. He's pretty sure we're in the first contingent going for invasion training and he swore it meant we'd be the first ashore when they do put on the invasion. I said I supposed someone had to go first, but he didn't find that very funny. In fact I'd heard a strong rumour going around here that there wasn't going to be a Second Front this year (like there wasn't last year). It was just a scare story put round by Churchill to frighten the Jerries. But Jack's quite sure of it. He reckons the whole operation has already been planned in detail down to the day and hour when we land on enemy soil. He says it's going to be Denmark. Landing in force by parachutes and landing-craft and drive south towards Hamburg. I'd have thought it would be easier to invade France, but apparently the German defences along the coast are too strong to be breached.

29 JANUARY

They don't seem to know what to do with us. Most people are out on the lawns sunning themselves. I'm alone in this extraordinary room. Instead of palliasses there are proper beds, like hospital beds, positioned between the mirrors and alcoves on opposite sides against the wall; the walls and ceiling are plaster and there are little plaster cherubs in the corners. The ceiling is very high and painted pale blue. As a concession to the parquet floor the Army has actually put little muffs on the bedlegs, or maybe it was the owner who did that before leaving for her estates in Scotland. We don't know who it was, but she must have been very rich. The black-out curtains in the downstairs rooms were made in velvet.

We are somewhere on the South Coast. It could be anywhere from Kent to Cornwall, but the general opinion is that it's Dorset. It will be easier to tell when we see the beaches. If there are any. It must have been about 10.30 last night that we finally arrived at a railway station (nameless) that was different from the rest. Instead of getting out, stretching our legs, getting a cup of tea and something to eat and then getting back in the train, we were out for good. The NCOs marched us down the road by torchlight to what looked like a deserted bus station. There was a drizzle of rain and no moonlight to see by. We stood easy, holding our rifles and wondering where we were, what we were doing and what the point of it all was. After a while the first of a convoy of trucks came out of the night and waited with its engine running long enough for us to clamber aboard. The inside stank of grease and wet serge. None of us said a word. We were too tired to speak. After six or seven miles the truck left the main road and turned sharply left through some tall gates. For several hundred yards we continued slowly up a narrow unmade road, the trees brushing against the canvas. The house, when we got out, looked enormous. The size of the Natural History Museum, with wings and turrets and balconies in all directions. A single light burned by the front door, up some grand stone steps. I hoped to find an ancient butler with grey hair and a stoop, but it was the usual officer with a clipboard who lined us up in the hall. Just behind where I was standing was a small lobby. The kind of place you store umbrellas or footmen. On the wall was a bell indicator with room-names beside the bell-pushes in old-fashioned lettering. 'School Room', 'Flower Room', 'Miss Eliza's Room', 'Billiard Room', 'Gun Room', 'Conservatory' and so on. Of course the Army had taken all the names off the doors and replaced them with numbers, but I think it must be the Ballroom that I'm writing this in. Our section was one of the luckiest. Upstairs they're having to sleep on palliasses and Jack was saying this morning that there isn't enough straw to go round.

Another unit is arriving tonight. Until then they've obviously decided to let us lie about and rest. Even the roll-call wasn't until 0900 hours. I'm surprised they didn't give us breakfast in bed. In the morning light the house looks smaller and a bit shabbier, but it's still a hell of a place. Two full platoons paraded on the gravel in front of the house and the CO gave us the news we'd been expecting. We're here to join 'other Allied Forces' in combined exercises and assault training. We start tomorrow morning. There was a south wind blowing as we fell out. I could hear the sound of the sea.

30 JANUARY

Down to the beaches in the morning. A mixture of pebbled shoreline and rocky coves with small inlets guarded by jagged outcrops of rock. If this is the sort of terrain we're going to be assaulting, heaven help us. Jack took one look at it and said it made Gallipoli look like a walk-over. We waited around all day for landing-craft to turn up. None arrived. Instead we had to practise cliff assaults. Ropes were tied to grappling hooks and fired to the top of the cliffs. The first two I watched couldn't find any support and came down as soon as the NCO started tugging. The third one seemed to be lodged safely but began slipping when the first bloke was twenty feet up. Luckily he held on and it let him down gently. After that they moved the firing apparatus twenty yards along and it was more successful. Even so it was pretty scary. You are supposed to hold on to the rope with both hands and walk up the cliff-face like a fly. Fortunately there were plenty of footholds and the slope became less steeply vertical after the first twenty feet. At the top I found I could walk up quite normally. The second time I made a mistake and looked down. I was half-way up and the men below already looked remote and tiny. Nothing but air between us. My stomach turned and my head whirled. I lost my foothold on the rock and hung for a moment in mid-air clutching the rope with both hands and kicking into space. I shan't forget that moment. I held on to the rope so tightly that my hands are still raw and painful. I thought I was going to fall. Then somebody steadied the rope from below. I found a toe-hold and continued up. Even then I had to pull myself up mostly by my arms. My knees had started to tremble and my legs felt weak and useless. If we'd been asked to climb a third time I don't think I should be here writing this.

I found a letter from Bob waiting for me when I got back. He's certainly changed since he enlisted into the Sappers. His letters used to be full of gossip. He'd send funny cuttings out of newspapers. Now he writes curt, factual letters with a lot of technical stuff he knows will go over my head. He no longer writes about the past and the experiences we have in common. It's all about the War and his unit. I was thinking that he's doing it deliberately, distancing himself from me as if he can't afford any longer to have friends from the past. But I've just realized with a shock the sort of letters I've been writing to him and to Mum and Dad since I left home. They must seem exactly the same.

1 FEBRUARY

The coldest month of the year. Just the weather to go swimming in the Channel. As a matter of fact they've started us off quite gently. Yesterday a couple of big tank-carrying landing-craft appeared offshore, wallowing like grey walruses, and we were shipped out to practise 'advancing ashore under enemy fire'. That meant lining up in the empty hold while the craft revved up its engines and moved a few yards inshore. Then the bows opened and a rope was shot to shore and we walked into the water at a stately pace, letting the rope guide us in

Through a hailer on the beach came an upper-class voice asking us to 'disembark as quickly as possible'. As if any of us were likely to hang about in cold water up to our necks! But it isn't easy to run through deep water in full kit with a rifle to keep dry. Jerry could pick you off and still have time for a mouthful of sandwich between shots.

Next, it's going to be the little assault landing-craft which rams up to the beach and pushes us out to sink or swim. Then they're going to put a complete operation together with LCAs and LCTs going in simultaneously. Tanks on the beach. Mines in the sand. Live ammunition whistling past our ears. And the cliff to climb at the end of it. To keep us in training and get us used to the idea of drowning with dignity, we've been promised a few rowing-boat landings among the rocks. Though if we're blown that far off course on Invasion Day we'll be lucky to get a Third Front going, let alone a Second one.

SAME NIGHT

The house is quiet. Most people have gone to the dance in the village hall. There's one the first or second Saturday of the month and the Army gives us late leave. Arthur asked me to go along with him. I said I didn't feel like it. I want time to be alone. Maybe I spend too much time alone. Protecting myself. I don't want to think too much about things outside, I want to get this thing finished. I want to be able to put it aside. And when it's over, say this was my life then and this is my life now. Does that make any sense? Probably not. After all, I've been to dances before. I've been home on leave. But it's different now. I've got a feeling that this is the final stage. I want to approach it with everything I've got, not be distracted. What difference is a village-hall dance going to make? I'm frightened all the same.

51

This house, on the other hand, I have begun to feel at home in. There's a history about it. It doesn't seem to matter that half the furnishings have gone and it's crowded with people. It accommodates us as gracefully as a luncheon party in the old days that you see photographs of. Must be something to do with the proportions. Upstairs is a corridor of locked rooms. Jack's unit found one with a key on the lintel. Inside was a complete child's nursery, with toys and games as if the children had never gone away. Many of them were old and beautifully made. There was a Victorian rocking-horse with a saddle painted on it in brown. And there were two amazing dolls' houses obviously made by hand, with the furniture and costumes designed down to the smallest detail. I don't know what the makers would have thought to see a squad of fully-grown soldiers treading gingerly round these objects, which looked even more miniature in our presence. Something struck me about the bigger dolls' house. In one of the downstairs rooms there were alcoves along the walls and tiny cherubs in the corners of the ceiling. I suddenly realized I was looking at a scale model of the house itself, delicate and exquisite in every detail. Just as I was about to look at it more closely an NCO appeared in the doorway and ordered us out. What followed next I shall relate in case the owner ever reads this. One of the lance-corporals, a big sullen brute from Glasgow, picked the dolls' house up in his arms. I don't know why. Perhaps he wanted to show it to the NCO or take it out as a keepsake. When he got to the door and the NCO told him to put it down, he dropped it. Simply dropped it on the floor. It cracked open from top to bottom and the pieces lay on the floor as we marched out and down the corridor.

My favourite room, which I have only seen once, is the library on the first floor. Normally I wouldn't have seen it at all since it's in the officers' section of the house. In fact I think it is the officers' mess together with the study next door. I had to take Captain Freeman a pair of binoculars he lost on the beach. Nothing can have changed. The books are still there ranged on their walnut bookshelves around the walls. In the middle is a lovely old beautifully polished round wooden table with a Chinese vase on it. While I waited for Freeman I went to look out of the bay window. There was a view over the lawn with clumps of trees sloping down towards the sea in the distance. It was like being in the Hall in *Random Harvest* with the old soldier come back to recapture the past. It was very peaceful and dignified. Out at sea a cruiser was passing. For a moment I thought 'this is what we are fighting for – this is what we are fighting to save'. Of course I soon remembered that this room, this house, this view, wasn't what most of us are fighting for at all. Captain Freeman came in, took the binoculars, and chucked them on the table. I left.

2 FEBRUARY

Arthur came back last night and said he'd pulled a girl three times in twenty-eight minutes in the bushes behind the village hall. I asked what her name was and he couldn't remember. Sometimes I don't think we're fighting the same War as Greer Garson.

4 FEBRUARY

Arthur reckons he's lucky to still be around. He nearly copped it this afternoon. Needless to say the smaller landing-craft still haven't arrived. We filled in time by the Sergeant organizing what he called a 'Commando Raid' in dinghies on a rocky part of the coast. I'm wary of the description 'Commando' ever since what happened to Vincent. I was very nearly proved right. It had rained all night. There were strong winds and the sea was rough. We went on board one of the transport craft and got into two large dinghies which were lowered from davits. I was in one, Arthur was in the other. Even before we cast off we were drenched. Arthur's boat was blown to the left. We could only just make it out in the driving rain. Ahead, the water thundered on the rocks. I can swim quite well, but I wouldn't have liked to have gone overboard in this weather. 'If I'd wanted this, I'd have joined the Navy,' someone shouted.

To the right of the narrow inlet, hardly big enough to take one dinghy let alone two, was a low jutting outcrop of rock sheltering a tiny anchorage. More by luck than good judgement we nosed against it. The Sergeant jumped with the rope on to the slippery rock and managed to make us secure. We all jumped for dear life. Bob Young slipped and slid back into the water, but we were all so wet by then it made little difference. We hauled the dinghy up and away from the worst of the battering and then watched as the other boat came in.

It made for the inlet below us. The water boiled up in it every time a large wave found its way in and surged out in a mass of white foam. The boat made the entrance and was carried in on the crest of a wave. The rocks sloped up on either side and in front of them. Arthur, in the front, saw a place to fasten the rope and got ready to jump. But an NCO grabbed the rope and jumped first. As he struggled to disentangle the rope we saw a wave break over the dinghy, followed by a huge swell. There was nothing anybody could do. It lifted the dinghy and its crew up like a matchstick and carried it up the inlet, with the NCO hanging on to the bowsprit, and dashed it against the rock. It overturned. The squad were thrown into the water and struggled to keep afloat in the foam and surge. Arthur and another bloke got hold of the NCO, who was obviously in pain, and pushed him across the hulk of the upturned dinghy. I don't know what any of them would have done if the Sergeant hadn't run back

54

to our boat and collected a second coil of rope used for emergencies. We threw it down to the swimmers and one by one they came ashore. The last two helped the Corporal, who had a badly bruised back. Arthur had enough left in him to ask the Sergeant if he had an umbrella. But he's looked completely flaked out all evening and I'm not surprised.

5 FEBRUARY

Assault training in LCAs. They give me the creeps.

7 FEBRUARY

The same dream two nights running. I'm standing in a landing-craft shoulder to shoulder with the rest of the squad. There is no sound. The sea is calm. Nobody moves. I look round and see Arthur and Jack standing behind me. I say something, call out to them, to break the silence. They don't answer. Their faces don't move a muscle. Just as I realize that I am the only one left alive there is a juddering roar of engines and the landing-craft surges violently forward. 'Hold tight to ram the beach!' somebody yells. I get ready to run for it. But I can't move. I am pinioned by all the bodies around me. In a panic I try to struggle free. The craft hits the beach with a jolt. The ramp falls. I plunge into the water, every muscle straining. At the same moment I get a terrible feeling of loneliness. I know that the men behind me were trying to hold me back. I tread on the sand. One step. Two steps. Breathing hard. My legs are weighed down like lead. Everything happens with agonizing slowness. There is a loud crack, the snapping sound a tree makes when it's felled. I see the bullet. I fling up my arms. My rifle flies away in a slow curve like a bird. My knees buckle. My head jerks back, losing my helmet. I suck in air desperately. My kit drops off one shoulder and opens, spilling its contents. My mess tin appears to fly past me. I feel the blood trickle down my face. It takes minutes to blink. I pitch forward very slowly. My knees hit the sand at the same moment as my rifle. As I fall, face down, I hear the others, the ones who waited, come running past. Their boots pound the sand like heartbeats getting slower and slower, further and further away. The last thing I notice is my shaving-brush lying by my head in the sand.

I wake up sweating. Last night it was even more vivid. I couldn't go back to sleep. I lay awake thinking, this is how it is going to be. I sat up in bed. It was the early hours of the morning. The room was dark and completely quiet except for the rustle of someone turning over in his sleep. If I had read about this happening to someone in a novel, I would have expected them to be groaning with fear when they knew suddenly and certainly as I did that they were going to die. But sitting up in bed and looking round at the sleeping forms on either side, it wasn't like that at all. I had a sense of total superiority. I knew something which they didn't. I had been given an insight into the future. I had been selected to be someone who knew he was going to be killed.

I got up, put on my coat and walked down the central gangway to the door. Of these people sleeping here some will be dead before the War is over. Bob Young perhaps, or Arthur. But unlike me, death will come as a surprise to them. They will not have prepared for it. Outside, there was a crescent moon in a deep-blue sky. The lawn was white with February frost and the grass crackled under my bare feet. From the evergreens between the garden and the sea came a sweet pine-wood smell. I formed the thought, you are going to die. The moon stayed where it was. The grass went on crackling under my feet. I went back inside and woke up in time for roll-call this morning.

9 FEBRUARY

A fine day. Cold but fine. Went for a walk with Jack this afternoon. We went out the north end of the grounds through some fields and up the hill behind. Saw a red squirrel and chased it up a tree. It carefully chose a branch just out of our reach and sat on it scornfully while we jumped as high as we could to try and frighten it. Thought of telling Jack about my dream and decided not to. After all, what do you say? The important thing wasn't the dream but the knowledge that came with it. I can explain the dream but I can't explain how strong was the realization that came too. And to say, as if conversationally, during an afternoon's stroll on the South Coast, 'I am going to be killed in the assault,' doesn't make sense. It doesn't fit in with the weather, the birds singing or the farm smells. What would Jack have said? He'd have said I was being superstitious. Privately he would think that I had lost my nerve.

Instead he talked about North Africa. There was plenty of death there. You didn't only have dreams about it. His unit had overrun a German advance position. It had been mortared but refused to surrender. Short bursts of machine-gun fire were pinning them down. Eventually the Lieutenant ran in under covering fire and chucked a grenade. The machine-gun went silent. They stormed the position and Jack was first to get there. Two of the Germans seemed to have been dead for several days. They were beginning to stink in the hot sun. One of them appeared to be breathing and Jack went over to investigate and found that his stomach had split open and things were crawling in the decay. The machine-gunner must have been wounded in the first mortar attack. Half his leg had been blown away. He'd wrapped his shirt around it, but so much blood and pus had seeped through that the shirt had matted into the wound and become part of it. Unable to reach water and delirious with pain, the boy (he was about eighteen, Jack thought) had inched over to the machine-gun and fired off short bursts to signal for help. A pity he'd been firing in the wrong direction. The grenade had taken off part of his scalp and thrown him on top of the machine-gun, hugging it like a baby. After a while the boy opened one eye. He said 'Hallo'. The Lieutenant shot him through the head, and they moved on.

We were on the road uphill by now. A vicar in black gown and dog-collar came past on his bicycle. He said Good Morning. We said Good Morning back. Although come to think of it, it was mid-afternoon. Jack said that after a time one death became very much like another no matter what the circumstances. Sometimes it came quick and neat, sometimes slow and painful, sometimes plain gruesome. Especially in tank warfare, where a shell could rip a tank apart or turn it into an oven. He'd seen men half burnt alive scramble clear with their clothes in flames and roll on the sand until they lay still. On the road to Tunis he'd held a dying German in his arms. And dying British too. He'd felt as angry and sorry for both. Dying people don't know what they're fighting for, Jack said, and right then you don't either. It wasn't long after the German gunner that Jack's Lieutenant copped it. He was leading the squad, advancing along a narrow ravine, and trod on a mine. The metal took away most of his stomach wall and a bit of intestine. They carried him for miles. He'd given them firm instructions never to give water to a man with a stomach injury so they tried to ignore him when he begged and pleaded for water. At last he started cursing them and saying they were trying to torture him to death and deserved to die with him. They couldn't go on any longer. So they stopped and gave him a drink from their water-bottles. He died soon after that.

I can see why Jack must be pissed off with our simulated battle training. But he doesn't go on about it. He's a better soldier than I could ever become. He's got the imagination, but he doesn't let it get him down. He doesn't brood like me, he's more stoical, he accepts that he's an obedient part of the war effort. If he gets through, so much the better. If he knew what I know, would he be so calm and stoical? The answer is that he would have to be a different person.

Walking down the other side of the hill into the valley we came to a strange sight. The road we were on led to a big stone farmhouse surrounded by barns and outhouses. In the yard outside the front door was piled a mass of furniture. Beds, tables, chairs, clothes, crockery and a copper hip-bath. The farmer and his two sons were loading the heavier stuff into two trucks. The farmer's wife was packing the kitchen and bedroom things into the boot of an Austin. A sheep-dog was racing round them, barking furiously. Jack and I went over to see if we could help and they said No, very curtly. 'It's a bloody invasion,' one of them said. For a moment I thought they meant Hitler, doing a surprise landing on the Dorset coast. But what had happened was they'd had an official notification from the Army announcing that the farm was going to be requisitioned 'temporarily' for the accommodation of Allied forces. A detachment of GIs is due to arrive tomorrow. As soon as the farmer (seeing we weren't American) started talking to us and telling us of the other houses hereabouts that have already been turned into billets, I began to see what he meant about a whole community disappearing. Soldiers are everywhere, driving in jeeps, flying in the sky, walking the roads in bizarre uniforms, hopping out of tanks, filling the pubs. The local people might as well have gone into burrows for all we see of them. For these people there really has been an invasion. And not always a 'friendly invasion', as it's called in the newspaper. The farmer's wife was crying. 'I know what those French feel now,' she said. Jack and I decided we'd come far enough and turned back.

Anyway it was starting to feel colder.

12 FEBRUARY

Rough seas for landing-craft training. The unlucky ones are in the middle. The lucky ones can be sick over the sides. I was one of the unlucky ones.

14 FEBRUARY

Arthur read out a funny story this evening from one of the magazines. This serviceman called Harold is telling his mum about landing-craft assault training in letters home. 'Dear Mum. Yesterday the order of the day was LCA training followed by artillery practice out to sea. There was a thick fog and my landing-craft got stuck on a mud-flat. No one noticed and we got shelled for fifty minutes by the shore batteries. Then the O/C of the training exercise realized he was an LCA short and sent an LCT (landing-craft, transport) out to look for us in the fog. The LCT hit us astern, got holed below the water-line, and sank rapidly. They had to wait for high tide and send out a cruiser to pick us all up.' When Arthur finished reading we all sang three verses of 'I Do Like To Be Beside The Sea Side' and would have sung several more if we hadn't been interrupted by gale-force winds blowing open the door, which we had to prop up with a chair.

18 FEBRUARY

Weather, which has been bad for the last week, improved enough this morning for the Army to bring out on display their new tanks specially adapted for beach warfare. All the top brass came down to watch the new toys being put through their paces. Some of them we'd seen before while they'd been on trial here. The flail tank, for instance, with flails on the end of two long attachments at the front, used for exploding ground mines and beating down coils of barbed wire. Also a track-laying tank which holds a round bale of canvas or something and lays a firm surface across soft ground. Most of us weren't watching very carefully, but craning round to try and see Monty, who was supposed to be the guest of honour. The trouble is he's quite short. When he isn't standing on a box making a speech he's usually surrounded by tall, stout, high-ranking officers who shield him from view.

I hope they shielded him effectively when the next display was put on: amphibious tanks that swim to shore from the LCTs. Three made it all right, but the last one sank in a cloud of bubbles and the crew had to make an emergency escape. They shot up like corks out of a bottle. The star attraction (what Arthur, who's been reading a textbook called *Polish Up Your French*, said was a *pièce de résistance*) was described as a Panjandrum. It came fizzing out of the LCT like a giant Catherine wheel. A rocket was attached to the end of each of its struts and impelled it along in the water like a hoop bowled with an invisible stick. When it got to the shore it wheeled around, canted drunkenly and finally fell over just in front of the photographers and film cameramen, who were clicking away like mad. Unlike the others, the Panjandrum seems to have no apparent purpose at all and no one can tell me what it is going to be used for. Unless it's to stun the Jerries with admiration for our efficiency so that they drop their weapons and surrender. It couldn't have mines attached to it, in case it wheeled round in the water and blew our own lot up. While we were thinking about it, Monty clambered up to a place where he was visible and made a speech to us. The wind was up by that time and blew some of his words away, but it was a speech to the effect that a nation which can invent such wizard toys must be bound to come up trumps against a nation which can't think up anything better than building a wall to keep us out. I am sure we all came away glad to know that we are now invincible and don't have anything to fear from the Huns, the Wops, the Nips or anybody else.

24 FEBRUARY

Tomorrow is the first full-scale combined assault exercise. The craft were already assembling this afternoon. The armour was loaded on and it looks very impressive. We were lined up by platoon on the beach and Johnson stalked up and down, warning us what to expect in the way of hidden mines flanking a corridor which we have to run down towards the cliffs. Johnson loves this kind of thing. He's one of the worst bastards among the NCOs. Like most redheads he's got very fair skin and when he gets narked he flushes up so strongly that it camouflages his sideboards. A fortnight ago he got so red and excited tearing a strip off one of his Corporals that an officer who was passing thought he was having a fit and asked him if he was all right or if he wanted to go and lie down. Since then we've been asking him very politely about his health and the other evening in the NAAFI when he came in, Arthur waited until he was close by and then said to me in a loud voice. 'You're looking a bit pale, Tom, why don't you go and lie down for a few months?' We fell about laughing. Johnson pretended not to notice, but he went bright red. I don't fancy Arthur's chances if he ends up under his command.

25 FEBRUARY

It went wrong from the start. There was a steady drizzle all day and a gusty wind from the sea. We were marched down to the quay and had to wait for an hour on the hards while tanks were taken on board the LCTs. One of them, following too closely on the tank in front, was made to stop suddenly going up the ramp. On the slippery surface it slid back a few feet, knocking down an engineer who'd been standing behind it. I saw it happen. So did the rest of the squad, but there was nothing we could do. It was over in a moment. The man went down with a cry and the tank went over his leg. The man pushed himself up into a sitting position and looked with surprise at where his leg had been. When the tank moved forward again and he saw what was left he began screaming and screaming. There was nothing there except a flattened jelly of blood and bone-splinters with a flap of trouser leg sticking out. A doctor came and gave him a shot of morphine and then spent a long time cutting him loose from the deck. When they put him on a stretcher and carted him past I could see his face. It was grey. In the background they were washing the remains of his leg off the deck with a hose. I never heard whether he lived or died. All I heard was that he was a local man with a wife and three children who had been a fisherman before the morning Hitler woke up and decided to invade his neighbours.

We got on board and steamed through a moderate swell towards the beach chosen for the exercise. There had been reports of E-boat sightings, so we kept close inshore, which delayed us further. Our objective was a hamlet a few hundred yards back from the top of the cliff, which I think must have been specially evacuated for our assault. By the time we had the beach ahead of us, the bombardment ships and rocket ships had already finished 'softening up' the target and were heading back out to sea. That created more confusion. Finally the ship manoeuvred itself into the right position, comfortably within range of enemy guns, had there been any, and we started clambering down the netting into our assault landing-craft.

Here we had the second casualty. Gregory, a quiet, unshowy bloke who sleeps four beds down from me, broke his ankle jumping into the boat. We'd never practised on the netting in a heavy swell before. The craft was rising and falling sharply. I'm surprised there weren't more of us hurt. Anyway we had to take Gregory in with us and the noise of him moaning, added to the pitch and toss of the LCA, was enough to give us all the heebie-jeebies.

Because of the weather conditions the LCA pilot bravely decided not to take us right up to the beach, but to let us swim for it. The ramp must have gone down in about five feet of water. As it did so I got the feeling, even worse than usual, of sheer blind panic. Knowing that I'm going to drown or get sucked under because my legs won't carry me to shore. This time they nearly didn't. I jumped and landed in icy green water up to my shoulders. The weight of my pack ducked me right under. I suddenly knew that if I fell, I wouldn't be able to get up. The thought of Vincent flashed through my mind. He must have felt the same thing. Known the water blacking out his vision, pouring into his mouth and the burden on his shoulders pressing him down, pressing him down ... so I didn't fall, I stood upright, the water cascading off me, gasping for air – and found the whole thing had happened in a split second. I hadn't even got the barrel of my rifle wet.

There was no time to think. Orders blared out at us to keep moving, keep moving up the beach. Some DD tanks had got there ahead of us and were firing their guns off aimlessly towards the cliff. I had no way of knowing if the LCA had landed us in a minefield or in a safe corridor. The only thing to do was to move up in between the flail tanks, trying to keep out of the way of the flying chains. The Army devised another game for us on the way to the cliffs. A line of hidden mines scheduled to give us enough time to reach the cliffs before detonating. Since we were advancing more or less as a unit, these didn't worry us. Rockets had already fired netting up to the top and we began climbing. Rain had made the ropes slippery. Several people fell off on the lower rungs and had to start again more carefully. Then Bob Young, who was climbing next to me, looked over his shoulder and shouted out. I stopped and looked back. A stretcher party had hoisted Gregory out of the LCA and were carrying him up the beach, obviously believing that the flail tanks had cleared the whole area. They were walking diagonally away from the shoreline. We watched, knowing what was going to happen next and as helpless to intervene as we had been on the hards. They had gone about ten yards when there was a bright flash of light and an explosion of sand. The front stretcher-bearer fell heavily, bringing down the other one and catapulting Gregory on to the sand. I looked at Bob and mimed that we should go down and help them. He nodded agreement. Just then a voiced floated up at us from below. It was Johnson, ordering us to keep moving and catch up the others, who were near the top of the cliff. He'd seen the explosion and he couldn't give a damn. He had his orders and he was there to see we carried them out. If we'd come down that cliff we'd have gone straight to solitary. We turned and carried on climbing. Writing this now at the House, I see Gregory hasn't come back and I'm not expecting him to. I asked Jack about the mines. He thinks they were probably thunderflashes, making a big explosion but not causing injury unless you step on top of one. I think it was a full-size land-mine, the sort we were threatened with before the exercise began. If Gregory's bed stays empty, I reckon I'll have been proved right.

Another bed is empty in this room tonight. On this one they have already changed the sheets and moved the personal belongings from the bedside locker. I watched them doing it, not with anger, but with curiosity. Two orderlies came in the same time as the first of us started filtering back from the exercise. Quickly they stripped the bed, folded the bedclothes and replaced them with newly-laundered ones. Opening the bedside locker, they swept all its contents into a plastic bag with a neat cardboard label. In less time than it takes to wash one's face a whole identity had been erased, scrubbed out of the world as if it never existed. In its place – a blank space waiting to be filled. A cog is needed. A drop of oil to service the machine. Who will come forward? For the first time I found myself hoping that it wouldn't take long. A blank bed is like a rebuke. It reminds me that somewhere there is somebody who hasn't yet learnt how to become a victim.

It was his fault. It's not my job to make excuses for our training instructors, least of all in this diary, but they did warn us. On the assault run from the cliff-top to the hamlet they would be firing over our heads to force us to keep low and use cover. Just to emphasize the point they would be using live ammunition. Better a few should die now than a whole lot later for lack of basic training. Or, as the officer put it afterwards, you can't make an omelette without breaking eggs. Play up, play up, and play the game. It was, mind you, still raining. The wind was whipping up the collar of my battledress. The hamlet was vaguely *over there* and a bit closer to *over here* was our particular objective: a summer-house set among low trees. In between was ugly scrub, a few stunted trees and various convenient hollows in the ground. We'd had the sea game. This was the land game. If you could get out of the bunkers and on to the green in five movements, it was an easy putt for victory.

Ducking low and weaving from side to side, as we've been taught to on God knows how many exercises, I ran for the cover of a wind-break of gorse bushes facing out towards the sea. Bob Young was just ahead of me. Tall and quick on his feet, he prefers to make straight for wherever he's going without bothering to crouch low. Cocktrotting, he calls it. Even so he's a bit slow today and we arrive at the bushes at the same time. The hamlet is already under fire. Smoke is rising from one of the far buildings. Looking across the broken terrain we can see small khaki figures popping out of holes, scuttling a few yards in the open and dropping out of sight. The gun-fire is continuous. At first we think it comes from our lot. But it doesn't. The bullets are too close for that. One has just gone singing overhead. Bob and I look at each other. The rumour is true, though we'd never believed it. The training instructors have taken up positions on either side of the assault course and set up a cross-fire with live ammunition to force us to keep our heads down. It isn't going to be easy.

Bob and I discuss things in a hurried whisper. He's all for going straight across the scrub and open ground, making a bee-line for the summer-house. 'Let's get the sodding thing over with,' he says. I don't fancy the idea of frontal assault. On our left, the gorse wind-break turns into a hedge running along the side of a field overgrown with weeds and tall grass. At the far end is a ditch lined with trees – a stream perhaps – which runs into the copse around the summer-house. We agree to go our separate ways. I crawl alongside the gorse hedge into the grassy field. The rain has turned the ground to mud but I daren't show my head because the bullets are still coming over. In the field, the grass is high enough to let me cover the ground quite fast, crouching low and jogging forward in a version of Bob's cocktrot. At the top of the field, the line of trees borders a stream, as I'd thought. I stand up and look across the assault course. A bullet sings past and snaps off a branch further along, but this time I don't duck. I'm watching Bob running towards the summer-house. He appears to be running quite slowly, in a completely straight line, disregarding all cover. As if he was running along a road in peacetime to catch a bus. Suddenly he throws up his hands and disappears. I breathe a sigh of relief, he's using ground shelter after all. Then he reappears. There's something odd about him. I've never seen Bob without his rifle. He treasures it. But now he seems to have thrown it away. He's holding

67

both hands to his head and slowing to a walk. Blood is coming through his fingers and gushing out of his mouth and nose. He walks a few more steps, then sinks to his knees and topples sideways. I can't see him any more. What I can see, however, turning round, is the outlines of a training instructor on the hillside. He has a gun and is reloading it. Steadying my rifle between two branches I get him in my sights. Then I press the trigger. I don't kill him, unfortunately. We have been issued only with blanks. After all, this is a training exercise. I carry on, splashing down the stream. Plenty of cover now. I race up and flatten myself against the wall of the summer-house. Edging round to a window with a dud grenade, I pull out the pin and throw it inside. In my squelchy boots I pound round to the front door, kick it open and throw myself inside. Arthur and a couple of others are sitting on the floor playing cards. The game is over.

26 FEBRUARY

Headachy. Running a temperature. MO called. Can't concentrate to write more.

28 FEBRUARY

Had a fever all Wednesday and yesterday. It came and went as suddenly as that. Thursday evening I was in the sick-bay shaking and sweating and sick. This morning I woke up as right as rain. The MO kept me under observation in the morning and sent me back here after lunch to convalesce. He said it was a bad chill caught on the Tuesday training exercise. Perhaps it was, I wasn't going to argue. The sick-bay was full of Tuesday's casualties. Bullet-grazes, flesh-wounds, broken arms and legs. It could have been a field hospital at the front.

The one thing that made me feel a bit better was to see Gregory there on Wednesday having his ankle set. He told me that 'all the serious injuries' had been taken away for treatment at the big Army hospital several miles away. I remembered something I'd forgotten to write down on Tuesday night when I was already feeling sick and dizzy and had put it down to shock rather than fever. The sight that greeted us as we got close to the hamlet proper – a line of ambulances parked all along the road. Like ice-cream vans at Epsom on Derby Day. I don't say they shouldn't have been there. It was the cold calculation of it that took my breath away. Waiting to mop up the blood after the last whistle had blown.

The House is quiet again. As I best like it to be. The others are out at rifle practice. This is what Bob Young liked best. If it was target shooting he'd come back with cards peppered with bull's-eyes. The RSM had put his name down for Bisley later this year. We all reckoned he was international standard. Good enough to compete in the next Olympics, if there is one. Now, like Arthur said, his sights are set on higher things. It wasn't a good joke, but by Christ we needed it.

12 MARCH

Sometimes I wonder whether we're being trained as soldiers or as athletes. This afternoon Sergeant Johnson took our platoon to one of the few beaches round here with good white sand instead of pebbles. We were lined up at one end and told to take our socks and boots off. For more than an hour we were made to run up and down. Our bare feet sank into the soft sand. Johnson bellowed at us to move faster. By the end our legs were aching so much that we could hardly stagger back to the trucks. Lying in bed, I can still feel the ache in my calves. If a few seconds' speed is going to make that much difference they must be planning to land us right in the thick of it.

20 MARCH

News on the radio at lunch-time that the Germans have invaded Hungary. Apparently the first the Hungarians knew of it was parachute troops landing on airfields and taking over air communications. This is one of the methods we spent months learning how to prevent when we were on anti-invasion exercises last year. It seems extraordinary that the Hungarians weren't better prepared. Although I suppose that, knowing Jerry could invade directly across the frontier, they didn't take much trouble to find ways of defending themselves. The other news is that the British and American armies are still pinned down south of Rome and making heavy weather of the advance. Every time I start thinking the War is nearly over and all will be well, some new set-back comes along. It could go on until there is nobody left to fight.

25 MARCH

After the combined exercise on which Bob Young died, the instructors have become frantic about keeping us low on the ground. We were marched up to the waste land at the back of the training area. I don't know if it used to be part of a mine or a quarry but the locals must have been using it as a dump for years. It's full of nettles, thistles, old tin cans, bottles and shallow pits of water and mud. Anyway, we were made to crawl across this. Wriggle across would be a better description. Every time we stuck our arses up more than three inches, Johnson would come up and thump us with a stick. It went on for what seemed like miles. By the end of it my trousers were ripped and my hands were bleeding.

5 APRIL

Another week of the same routines. Square bashing, route marching, rifle practice, camp fatigues, landing-craft exercises, beach exercises, cliff assaults and the rest of it. Another week out of my life. Stuff we've been practising for weeks, months, sometimes years. There comes a stage when practice can't make any more perfect. I'm a long way from perfect, but doing the same thing over and over again isn't going to make me any better than I am now.

Jack doesn't agree. He says that a soldier can learn something with his brain until he knows it backwards, sideways and upside-down. But under fire, in the fog of war, his mind is likely to go a total blank. Not unless the training is dinned into his unconscious, so he does the right thing by reflex, is he going to survive the first fighting. That says a lot about the Army. If the top brass, like the rest, have been trained to act according to their reflexes, no wonder we're in the mess we are.

12 APRIL

Janey. Janey. Janey. Janey.

13 APRIL

She was sitting by herself on a bench by the wall. Legs crossed, hands in lap, looking small and rather frightened. I wasn't feeling too good myself. I was still shaken up by Bob getting killed and a bit weak from the after-effects of the fever I'd had. But I'd half-promised Arthur that I'd go with him to the Saturday night dance and I couldn't very well let

71

him down again, seeing as it only happened once a month. It was raining, which didn't make me feel any better, particularly as those waterproof capes couldn't keep a mouse dry. Luckily we hitched a lift from the local doctor and got to the village hall quite early. That's probably the only reason I got to meet Janey. If the doctor hadn't picked us up, she'd have been snapped up in a flash by some randy GI from the American camp and that would have been the last anyone would have seen of her all evening.

Arthur really fancies himself on these occasions. I noticed he'd brushed his hair forward, and stuck a couple of flashes on his shoulder that I hadn't seen before. I asked him what they were. He said one was the Distinguished Servicing Medal and the other was Marksman (Shooting From The Hip) First Class, and the girls who didn't find that funny weren't his type.

It started off in the ordinary way, with me wishing I'd never gone. These things are so artificial they usually turn me right off. It's not that I'm nervous, but I look nervous and that makes me nervous. And I smoke a lot (must remember to return cigarettes to Arthur), which I don't normally, and that leaves me with a nasty taste in my mouth, so I drink more than usual too. The combination makes me feel sick before half the evening is out, by which time the best girls (the ones who were there when you arrived and you looked at and decided you'd wait for better ones to turn up, which they don't) have already been picked up. You're left to dance with the real skivvies or else go home, which you can't because you were given a lift by your friend, who is obviously getting places with a nice girl and is going to be here all evening.

That was how I felt going into this place, although it was well lit and cheerfully decorated with streamers and a few Fougasse posters round the walls. And *civilians*! It was like re-entering a forgotten world. A bit uneasy and polite. I went over to the bar with Arthur, who was going to ask for beers. A big blonde with swinging boobs under a red jersey caught his eye just then, so Arthur changes his mind and says casually, 'Got any wine, have you?' *'Wine?'* says the barman as if Arthur was some sort of freak from outer space. 'Two pints of brown, then,' says Arthur, but the barman had the last word. 'Vintage?' he asks sarcastically. The girl in the red jersey spluttered into her drink. Arthur turned pink and tapped his fingers on the bar. I felt a bit better and drank some beer. Arthur got talking to the blonde and I looked around the room.

I remember everything about the moment. Arthur was feeling the red jersey between his fingers ('My old man's in fabrics'). The band were tuning up. A couple of WAAFS had come in the door shaking off rain. Janey was over by the wall looking directly at me. I continued to gaze around the room as if nothing had happened, but my mouth went dry. I had another mouthful of ale and looked again to make sure I wasn't imagining things. I wasn't. She had lovely dark-brown hair drawn back tightly above her forehead and coming down in curls round her ears. Dark eyes (now looking away from me). A short straight nose and a wide mouth which was slightly down-curling in a look of boredom. It was difficult to tell how old she was because her dress was a bit old-fashioned (I can't remember if I knew that or if she told me later). It had a high neck with flounces at the shoulders. A beautiful gold-green summery pattern that made everybody else look dowdy.

I had another drink and looked for Arthur but couldn't see him. The amazing thing was that she didn't seem to have a man with her. I walked the long way round to give him a chance to come back from the toilet or from the bar with expensive drinks. To sweep her on to the dance floor, which is what usually happens. Nobody came, although I waited, so I said hello and she said hello. Instead of telling her she was the most beautiful girl I'd ever seen and I was in love with her face, her hair, her eyes, her dress and everything else, I asked her if she would like a drink, to which she said no, and had she been here long, to which she said about as long as most people I suppose. But she said it nicely, with a smile, and didn't even seem bored with such stupid, meaningless questions. In fact she asked me one back. 'How long have you been here?' she said, in a firm, soft, not at all girlish voice which I immediately added to all her other good qualities, and we went on from there.

When I say we went on from there, it took a little time to go anywhere. I don't know why I ever try to impress people by being casual at parties. Either it comes naturally like with Arthur or it's a waste of time. But I said in a bored voice that I didn't think I'd stay long and dancing was dull, didn't she think (in case she did). But she said in a decided tone that she didn't think dancing was at all dull, so I was trapped. I asked her if she wanted a dance. She said I don't mind if I do. The band was playing 'Let Him Go, Let Him Tarry'. The hall was full of people dancing and talking. The streamers were flapping and I had this smiling dark-curly golden girl in my arms and if anything else had ever mattered, it didn't any longer.

I told her my name, which seemed a good place to start. She said hers was Janey. It was too noisy to talk much. I wanted to concentrate on my dancing, which I've never been good at. Arthur came past with his drab and I was so pleased to catch the look of envy on his face that I stepped on Janey's shoe. She was kind about it, but I think she'd had enough by the time we'd finished. The band started up 'We Don't Know Where We're Going' and we stood there in silence for a moment. I knew that if I let her go and she went back and sat down on that bench, I would lose her. 'Shall we go outside for a bit?' I blurted out. She looked doubtful and asked, 'What for?' All I could think of was that the rain had stopped. What with the music and the black-out it was a pretty wild guess. Luck was on my side.

It was pitch-black outside and sweet-smelling after the rain. I thought of walking up the path behind the hall towards the churchyard, but Janey didn't have walking shoes on so we kept to the road instead. It was quiet, except for the dripping of the trees and an owl hooting somewhere. Janey turned up the collar of her heavy coat which made her look even smaller inside it. I clumped along beside her feeling large and unwieldy. She didn't say anything for a bit and I wondered if she resented being dragged out into the cold. Then she said, 'Have you seen any action?' I wasn't expecting that. It crossed my mind to pretend I was a battle-scarred veteran and tell her some of Jack's stories about North Africa. I said, 'Not really.' 'What do you mean, not really?' she wanted to know. So I told her a bit about training. I told her about the assault courses, about navigating dinghies in rough seas and about the mines and bullets that awaited us when we got to shore. I also told her about Bob Young.

I must have rambled on a bit, but she listened very intently holding on to my arm now as we walked up the road. At the end she asked, 'Do you like being a soldier?' I hadn't thought about it that way. Not since recruit training. I said, 'Not much, no.' 'Then why are you?' That was obvious, I'd been called up like everybody else. But she persisted. 'Is that all?' she wanted to know. Normally I would just have said yes. I don't find these direct questions very easy to answer. But I felt I was having to justify myself. I'd been talking to her about the danger, exhaustion and risk of death. What was it all for? I can't remember exactly what I said. 'It's got to be done,' I started feebly. Then something like, 'We've got to finish it off and pay out the ones who started it.' Did I mean to say that? Arthur would have had a good laugh. Officer-talk he would have called it. But what would he have said if Red Jersey had asked him the same question? Probably pushed her down in the grass and kept her mouth otherwise occupied. I decided it was time to change the subject.

I didn't know how though. I'm not like Arthur. I don't go for the one thing only. And Janey wasn't that sort of girl, it was plain to see. I hate these situations where you feel the wrong approach can ruin everything. Eighteen months ago I wouldn't have taken the risk, coward that I am. I would have nattered on about the War, the crops, the weather, anything except what I wanted to talk about. Last night I was a little bolder, but not much. 'I think you're very nice,' I said at last. She seemed quite surprised, so I said it again. 'I like you too,' she said. I like you too. Easy as that! I felt very grateful. I felt as if she had done something marvellous and self-sacrificing for me. All the obstacles were cleared away. I could tell her how nervous I'd been when I first talked to her (she knew that already) and how I hadn't really thought the dance dull (she probably knew that too but was too tactful to say so). That's when I should have taken her in my arms, embraced her and held her close, feeling her body through her coat and the summery-patterned dress. Instead I stopped walking and said very formally, 'Can I kiss you?'

She showed less shyness than I expected. 'If you want,' she said. So I kissed her. Her cheek was wet, I suppose with rain. When she kissed me back it was hardly more than the touch of a butterfly. I pulled her closer. She stopped me and moved away a bit. 'I've got to go now,' she said. And seeing my disappointment added, 'I'm with my brother, he's in the band.' She stood with her chin tilted, looking up at me. My thoughts were flooded with the urgency of seeing her again. Of not letting her slip away. I asked her. 'Whenever you like,' she said, 'except tomorrow.' And tomorrow is today and *tomorrow* I'll be seeing her! Six o'clock on that patch of road under the trees. She'll be waiting for me. Or more likely I'll be waiting for her.

I walked her back to the hall. The wind was slicing more coldly. The quiet was broken by the sound of bombers flying along the coast. The old loneliness came back, more sharply now with Janey beside me. 'I wish I'd met you before,' I told her. 'There's so little time now.' She stopped and looked at me. How is she to understand if I don't understand myself? She asked what I had said that for. I had nothing to tell her. Just a feeling, I said, and laughed. No more than that. I shan't forget her reply as long as I live. 'You'll be back,' she said. 'And there'll be time.' And then she kissed me. It wasn't a brush on the cheek this time but her face against mine, her lips and tongue, on and on endlessly, until the trees were swaying and the ground was swaying under my feet as if it wasn't earth at all but sea and the assault craft plunging towards its last harbour.

14 APRIL

Lousy day. The blister after this morning's route march has come up painfully. I can hardly walk across the room. God knows how I'll get up to the village. Letter from home asking why I haven't written. What do they expect me to do, write every day? An hour to go. What will I do if she doesn't come? I don't even know her last name. Just Janey.

I'll start out in ten minutes. It'll take me longer than usual to walk it. If I get a lift I can wait there for half an hour. Nine minutes.

15 APRIL

Didn't get a lift and spent forty minutes walking to meet Janey. Arrived and found that the road, in daytime, was a lot longer than I'd remembered. It curved round a bend. Had to walk up and down it a while. Janey came up behind me. She didn't touch me or call out, but stood there until I turned and saw her. We said hello, but it was awkward at first. She was even more pretty than I remembered from Saturday night. She'd seemed a bit pale then and tired. Now she was flushed. Her cheeks were red and her eyes were sparkling. She said, 'I'm sorry I'm late. Mum's upstairs with a cold and I had to check the till when we closed up.' I told her she looked beautiful, which was God's truth. She said, 'I've been running,' as if that's all it was. She had her hands deep in her coat pockets and her shoulders hunched against the cold. And she was smiling.

We didn't do much. Walked up towards the church. She talked a bit more about herself than she did the first time. Things are hard at the moment. Her dad runs the local tobacconist's, which also sells things like sweets and newspapers and elastic bands. They've been hit harder by the shortages than most people. Especially the tobacco shortage. I think she worries about it a lot.

It was easy to talk. For the second time in three days I left the Army behind me. I could feel some of the other life coming back to me. Like the blood tingling at the end of my cold fingers and toes. She hugged me closer. She likes me, I am sure of it. I don't know why yet. We walked through the churchyard, which was empty and peaceful. I brushed the earth off one of the gravestones. 'Alfred Charles Bottomley 1819–1883 May the Lord Preserve Him and Keep Him in Righteousness all his Days.' 'How horrid,' said Janey, 'to go to Heaven and find your old man preserved like a gherkin in a jam-jar with only a pair of wings to tell the difference.' We walked round the back of the cemetery to a piece of open ground with forty or fifty small wooden crosses. The crosses had no prayers or loving memories. Just names and dates. Corp. Jas Howarth 1890–1915. Sgt. Thomas Bellamy Singleman 1888–1915. Bombadier George Prebble 1900–1917. Old men, young men, fifty-year-olds, seventeen-year-olds, the flower of the parish, all killed in the Great War. And here we were doing the same thing all over again. The dead are real here. They rise up at you.

We left the place. I talked to Janey about the dolls' house done as a replica which we'd found in the nursery. She didn't say much at all. At the gate we said goodbye. I had to get back. Janey had to go home and cook her mother's dinner. I kissed her and held her tightly. She walked back through the trees, until she was out of sight.

16 APRIL

Bought three boxes of matches, two packets of sweets and a ball of string.

17 APRIL

Janey got the afternoon off. I was on fatigues until 3.30 — just my luck. I got hold of a bicycle and rode down to the shop. Janey was waiting at the back of the shop, just putting her coat on. Apart from the dance I don't know what she looks like without it. She was holding a brown paper bag, but wouldn't tell me what was inside it until we were out of the shop. Then she opened it. There were four scones inside! She'd just finished baking them, using up three days' butter ration. We went along the cliff road looking for a way down to the sea that didn't have Army Keep Out signs blocking the path. We found one, but decided it was too cold to go down. The beach was deserted. The sea was green and calm. As Janey said, nothing could look less frightening or dangerous. But as we stared at it, I suddenly seemed to see a sight Dad had told me about once, one of his stories about Gallipoli. The whine of shell-fire. The soldiers jumping out of pinnaces and struggling ashore. The bodies torn and crumpled at the water-line and the sea stained crimson with their blood all along the verge. Janey must have noticed my expression. She was quiet for a bit and then said, 'At the church, Tom, looking at those graves. What were you thinking about?' I told her about Dad's brother. I knew he'd died in the Great War but Dad had never talked about him. Not until I was home back on the last leave I had and got to talking about Vincent did he let on what had happened. He and his brother Tom had gone through the War together. They'd passed into the same regiment and fought side by side in the fields of Flanders. One morning in 1916, when their position was under heavy fire, Tom came up to my dad in the trench and gave him a letter. He said, 'Look after this, will you? I think you might be out of this before I am.' Dad thought it was a bit of a strange thing to say, but he took the letter and put it in his battledress. Tom went back down the trench towards his look-out position. He'd walked, said my dad, in a stiff, jerky way like a sleep-walker. Ten yards down the line a German shell got a direct hit. Dad was knocked sideways. Tom was underneath it. 'He was blown apart,' said Dad, the tears coming down his face. 'One moment he was there, the next moment he was no more.' Dad broke down and was taken into the dug-out. Before they had to beat a hasty retreat he was taken up and shown the grave they had dug for Tom, with a simple cross on it. They wouldn't tell him when he asked them whether they had found anything to bury inside.

I don't know why I tell Janey these things. It seems an odd way of going about a courtship. I talk to her about the little things as well. About the way she looks and how I think of her when I'm away from her. She says a few shy things back which I can take away and treasure until the next time. But the War comes between us. Or rather, it comes around us. Like a blanket, in which we huddle in the darkness and talk about what might be outside. She wants to know about the War and my feelings about the War. She said to me today, 'If you don't tell me, I'll never find out. And I need to know.' With Janey I want to forget about the War. But for her I *am* the War.

80

21 APRIL

On guard duty all last night. One bloke turned up at three in the morning after weekend leave. Said his girl was off abroad next week on an RAF posting. This had been the last chance he'd have to see her. I let him through without reporting him. If it's found out, I suppose I could be put on a charge. But I know that if the same thing had happened with Janey I'd have skipped camp all night.

24 APRIL

To see Janey at the shop. She took me upstairs to show me her room. 'That's nice,' I said, looking at the bed. She laughed. 'The shop's right underneath, I don't think Mum would stand for it,' she said. I was amazed. I thought she'd have shied away at the least mention of sex. Once or twice before when I'd been kissing her and feeling for her breasts she'd taken my hands away; 'Not now, Tom, please.' I took her in my arms and kissed her. She half lay back across the bed. I think it excited her to be doing this with her mother below. As for me, I was as excited as hell. She let me put my hand up her blouse. Her nipples were hard, and she moaned a little. But as soon as I shifted to take her hand and bring it down between my legs, she slipped from under me and sat down at her dressing-table. I got up to go. She stopped me. She was breathing quickly and her cheeks were red. She said, her mouth pressed into my jacket so I could hardly hear her, 'Not here, not here.' But I knew she also meant 'Not yet, not yet.' Arthur would probably have taken her there and then. His view's always been, never look at the mantelpiece while you're poking the fire. Anything in skirts will do. He divides women into 'talent' and 'class', and it's the first category he's talking about. Janey's class. And

I think I'm in love with her. So we went downstairs and had a cup of tea instead.

25 APRIL

I hate the bloody Army. I was due for a weekend pass tomorrow. I'd told Janey. We were going to get out of this coastal dump and I was going to take her to London, where she hadn't been since her dad took her up as a little girl to see the Christmas decorations. I'd saved up for it and Janey had spent hours getting her mum to agree. Now we've been told that all weekend leave is cancelled. Our Company and 'C' Company are going off on a forty-eight-hour map-reading exercise in the country. And next week my long leave falls due and I've promised to take it all at home. Janey was upset when I told her this evening. Her mother and brother were both at home so we could only have a few minutes alone. I thought of deserting for the weekend and coming back on Monday to take the consequences. But like Janey said, it would be the worst thing I could do. My long leave would be cancelled and I'd be put in solitary. Probably the adjutant would write home and explain why they wouldn't be seeing their son. And with new rumours every day about the Second Front, they'd start thinking I'd ruined their last chance of seeing me.

Arthur can't understand what I'm worried about. It's only a fortnight, he says, and you'll be in there again. It's all he thinks about. And in a fortnight's time we might be heading for Portsmouth or somewhere. Getting ready for the Channel crossing. Anything might happen.

29 APRIL

Got home late last night after a terrible journey, which took me nearly into Wales. All buses had stopped. I had to walk from the station through blacked-out streets I could hardly recognize. When I got in, Mum and Dad were waiting up for me with hot soup. Tina jumped around, barking as though the house was on fire. I suppose I should have been glad to see them. They fussed around me as if I'd come from the Front instead of from a Dorset training camp. But I hardly said a word. I drank my soup and went to bed. They thought it must be because I was tired after the journey. I was tired. But the truth is that all I could think about was Janey.

30 APRIL

Nothing much has happened here at home. I might as well have never been away. My mother has cut little bits of sound advice out of the newspaper and pasted them up in the kitchen. 'Badly-cooked cabbage loses its Vitamin C.' You don't say. The local rag has a spirited correspondence going about whether chiff-chaffs are scarce this year. One letter-writer says he has just come up from Surrey, where he was doing Government work on Leith Hill. Apparently there are plenty of chiff-chaffs on Leith Hill.

1 MAY

I meant to write before about the weekend exercise. Both Companies were given detailed maps and 'C' Company was detailed to retreat along a fixed route with our lot chasing them. I've always been quite good at map references and didn't find it too difficult. We set off as a platoon, using as first reference the roundabout on the Dorchester road, and then separated into sections. Arthur and I managed to lose the others along a railway cutting and went on ahead. This was the reverse of usual, but Arthur had a girl waiting for him in Wool and wanted to spend the night with her there. The alternative was a bivouac in a field, so I agreed to travel with him on condition he'd find me a bed to sleep in.

What we hadn't reckoned on was catching up the retreating Company, who'd had an hour's start on us. The first we knew of them was a thunderflash detonating a few feet behind us. We threw ourselves down and looked up in time to see two more thunderflashes lobbed over a wall at us. We picked them up and threw them back. Then we beat a hasty retreat in the opposite direction to let them carry on their retreat undisturbed. After a lengthy detour we got to the afternoon check-point not many minutes before the rest of the platoon was due. Tossed up whether to stay and bivouac or make for a comfortable bed. Decided to press on to Wool.

By the time we got there we were both dead tired. Arthur had been mysterious about the girl. When we found her flat, up above a chemist's in the main street, it turned out to be the girl in the red jersey from the village-hall dance. She was obviously put out to find two of us on her doorstep. Stinking, dirty and exhausted. She seemed to be in two minds whether to let us in at all. Arthur explained that I had nowhere to go and that without my map reading neither of us would have made it to the village. So she pulled us inside and went off rather crossly to the kitchen to make some cocoa. I realized to my horror that the room I was in was the only other room in the flat (unless I was to sleep standing up in the wardrobe). Arthur didn't seem to mind. He pulled the cushions off the sofa and laid them end to end on the floor with two at the top for a pillow. The girl, Angela her name was, came out with the cocoa and watched him. 'What's Tom going to do for blankets?' she asked, with a note of sarcasm in her voice. It was a very cold night. Arthur went to her wardrobe and began taking out a couple of her coats. Including an expensive-looking fur one. I sat and sipped cocoa. After what the diplomatic correspondents would call a heated discussion, Arthur put her coats back in the cupboard and the cushions back on the sofa. That was how it happened that on the night I'd hoped and intended to spend in bed with Janey in London, I ended up sharing a bed with Arthur and Angela, trying to get to sleep while they made love a few inches away. It may have been the bitter thought of that or merely tiredness after the day's exercise, but when Angela changed places with Arthur and in a motherly way put her arm round my shoulder, I laid my head on her generous and well-proportioned bosom and burst into tears. Immediately afterwards, in that comfortable position, I fell asleep. Much to the annoyance of Arthur on the other side.

5 MAY

Still home. One more week here. I thought of going south early, but they really are behaving as though they aren't going to see me again for years. Also I had the dream again last night. The details never change. Except that sometimes I see myself as if looking through the wrong end of a telescope, without the landing-craft or the sea or any of the others in the picture. Just me, in full uniform, running on the sand and being flung back in the air by some mighty force. Arms outstretched, helmet flying off, rifle thrust away and down into the soft sand, pillowing into darkness.

I've never told them about it. It would worry them too much. Especially Dad. He's taken the whole of this week off work. He wants to take me on some of the walks we went on when I was a boy. My coming back with news of invasion training has got him thinking for the first time in years of his own experiences. It's loosened his tongue. He's been coming up with amazing stories (none of them in Mum's hearing of course) that make me understand, as nothing did before, why he's kept silent about them so long. Gas, for instance. Something I'm never likely to have to face, unless the Japs are using the stuff. In Flanders, whenever the warning came, he had to put on something called a 'smoked helmet', which must have been almost as bad as the gas itself. Over his head he pulled thick yellow flannel all the way down to his shoulders and tucked into his shirt. It was saturated with a chemical supposed to repel the gas-effect. The transparent window for the eyes would get misted up almost at once and Dad described what it was like blundering blindly along a hole dug in the mud, stepping over dead bodies while the gas wafted over and the shells whined overhead. I wondered at first why he chose this time to tell me. I think I know now. It makes me feel less alone. Less alone even as a generation. And I know that whatever happens in Europe, supposing that the worst details of my nightmare come true, cannot be as much of a hell on earth as what my father has been through before me.

The other thing he tells me is that although he hated the War, hated the stupidity and pity of it all, he never managed to hate the Germans personally. His mates felt the same. The War was too big and inhuman for that, when you were in the middle of it. The real hatred was felt by civilians at home. I wonder if it will be the same this time? It certainly supports what Jack was saying about the North African campaign.

8 MAY

Postcard from Jack. He's been promoted to Corporal and attached to my platoon. No letter from Janey in answer to mine.

9 MAY

Postcard from Janey!

The actual postcard was glued into the pages of the Diary below this entry.

Dear Tom,

I got your letter. Thank you very much for your love and good wishes. I look forward to seeing you very much. All is well down here and quite sunny, except that Mum has got her cold back and I have been working like nobody's business.

Love and kisses,
Janey

I came down early as I've been doing all week to get the mail before Mum gets up. And there it was. How I love her! I'm counting the hours till I get back to the Army, which I never expected I'd do. Still, it's been a good rest.

11 MAY

Train very full. I've hardly got room to write. They both came to the station to see me off. I think they miss Michael a lot. Quite a number of kids who were evacuated four years ago have come back home, but Mum and Dad have decided that Michael should stay in Canada until the War's over. Mum was upset because it's my twenty-first birthday in six days. For some reason she kept on about it. 'How are we going to get things to you? What if the invasion's started and we don't know your address?' I thought of suggesting that she arrange to drop my cake by parachute. Instead I told her that next time I'm home I'll organize the biggest birthday party the street has ever seen. I had to shout it because the train was moving out. They stood together on the platform, suddenly looking small and frail. The next moment they were hidden behind a detachment of sappers who'd been marching on to the platform and that was the last I saw of them.

12 MAY

The Camp is buzzing with rumours that the invasion is about to get under way. These rumours have been going around for months, but the atmosphere is tenser than I can remember it ever being. A Company of Engineers who were billeted in the East Wing moved out over the weekend and our Adjutant was heard saying he didn't think anyone else was going to replace them. A mate of Arthur's who got leave to visit his parents in Dover came back saying that the hards are crowded with dummy landing-craft, painted grey, to fool the Krauts when they do aerial observation over the coast.

I'm writing this in the guard hut. I tried to have my name taken off the roster for tonight so I could get out and see Janey. Having just got back from long leave it didn't go down too well. I can't bear to think of her waiting for me, wondering if I've come back and if I still love her. I've been thinking about her all day.

13 MAY

Another fine sunny day. Orders to stay within bounds, but nothing for us to do. Jack says they'd planned another combined forces assault exercise for today, but all the landing-craft have suddenly been withdrawn to Poole. We were let out at six. I got a bike and went off straight away to the village with Janey's present from home in the saddle-bag. I rang the bell and waited. Janey's mum came to the door. She had been crying. She said hello and then said, 'Janey's not here. I'm sorry.' I had a sudden flash that she was dead. I remember thinking, 'I'm never going to see her again.' My legs went like jelly and I had to make a grab for the doorpost to keep upright. Then she was saying not to worry, Janey will be back tomorrow. She's gone to accompany her young brother, also called Thomas funnily enough, on his journey to camp for recruit training. Apparently Tom's call-up papers arrived while I was on leave. It's strange to think of blokes younger than me. Younger and younger all the time. Putting on their coat, picking up their suitcase and walking into the great sausage-machine.

I'm still inside it, so I don't know what comes out the other end.

14 MAY

At last. She'd left a message at the shop and was waiting for me on the steps of the Memorial at the edge of the village green. I held her very tightly. We had a lot to tell each other. She seemed tired and a bit edgy, but wanted to hear about Mum and Dad and the leave. She's never been north of Rugby or seen the inside of a steel foundry, so I don't think I was able to give her much idea of the atmosphere of the place up there. She said she had missed me. Thought of me every day. I thought this was a good moment to say I was getting a twenty-four-hour pass this Sunday and to ask her to spend the day with me in the country. She sounded very doubtful about it at first. But I told her it was going to be my birthday on Sunday and so she said yes. We walked and talked for an hour and went back to have tea in the room behind the shop when it started to grow dark. Janey's mum is still very upset by Tom leaving to join the Army so I didn't stay long. I told her it isn't as bad as all that!

15 MAY

Put on forty-eight-hour stand-by for moving Camp. It hasn't sunk in yet. After so many rumours and false alarms I can't properly believe it. I wrote a letter home and said it might be the last one they get from me for some while. I'm seeing Janey tomorrow.

17 MAY

I'm writing this in a bell-tent pitched in a field up above a small seaside town which must be nameless. The flap is open to let in the last of the afternoon sun. The light filters through the green canvas dimly as if we are living underwater. There are eight of us in here. Eight straw-filled palliasses on the bumpy groundsheet. The atmosphere is close. It smells of sweat, old socks and of course khaki. The army smell that never changes.

I shift to get in a better writing position and the straw crackles loudly in the enclosed space. With eight of us living here it will not be easy to get much sleep. Except for Jack, who's reading a paperback, the others are over at the NAAFI marquee. I'm feeling too sick at heart to join them.

The movement orders were confirmed late last night. By 0900 hours this morning we'd swept and scrubbed the barrack room and the ballsroom, as the Corporal calls it, which goes to show the sense of humour in this Camp. It could almost be used for dancing again. We'd cleaned out the stove in the middle of the floor, and lead-polished it as if it mattered. Took our folded blankets to the quartermaster's stores in the cellar and fell in on the gravel outside the porticoed front entrance. It looked a bit chipped and battered now, where we'd assembled three and a half months ago. It was all very sudden. I think everyone felt tense but thankful that at long last something was happening. Everybody except me.

The worst thing was that when we did get into the open trucks and set off for wherever we were going, we were driven through the village. The shop was open, but there was no sign of Janey inside. Upstairs, the curtains were drawn. I remembered what she'd said to me the first evening we'd met. 'You'll be back, and there'll be time.' We drove on, out of the village, lorryload after lorryload. It didn't feel like I'd be coming back.

We twisted and turned down country roads until I'd lost all sense of direction. Jack had found a comfortable seat in the corner. Arthur was leaning against the tail-gate, smoking. Like he said, it's a game of musical bloody chairs. 'Thousands of us moving around from camp to camp waiting for someone to shout "Second Front! Last one over's a Charlie!"'

First one over's a Charlie if you ask me. There we were, crowded into white-starred trucks on a fine morning in early summer. Bumping along Dorset lanes past quiet country woods and coppices that had never seen anything wilder than a cow. And now they were solid with invasion tanks and jeeps. Camouflage nets dropping from every tree. Jack was whistling the song that's become a theme tune for us in the last few months . . .

'We don't know where we're going until we're there,
There's lots and lots of rumours in the air,
We heard the Captain say,
We're on the move today,

91

We only hope the blinking Sergeant Major knows the
   way,
They've chased us round and round the barrack square,
And now we're on the road to anywhere,
No one's in the know,
We're singing as we go,
Oh, We don't know where we're going until we're there.'

You'd think they'd have a bit of sympathy for us by now.
That's what Arthur grumbled. Jack took his fag out of his
mouth and said a GI had told him where to find sympathy:
'It's in the dictionary between shit and syphilis.' Good old
Jack. The road to anywhere. Paris? Berlin? It doesn't seem to
matter. I felt the same as I had as a child watching in awe as a
procession of black hearses set off at funeral pace down
London Road towards the cemetery. Except that this time I
was in the front hearse.

It was an impressive sight though, I have to admit that.
Our convoy was halted at a level crossing. After a long wait,
an enormous locomotive came through, blowing hard. I
counted forty wagons before I stopped. On each one a brand-
new tank. Further on we passed a long line of tank-carrying
lorries, parked each side of the road. It was like driving down
a canal between walls of steel. Jeeps, lorries, tanks, armoured
cars. Each with the invasion star painted on the grey-green
metal. The White Star Line. The most expensive shipping
company in maritime history. And for such a short cruise too,
in all likelihood.

Sometimes the old world, the peacetime world, put in an
appearance. Once we were halted at a crossroads to let some
vast amphibious vehicles trundle by. A butcher's boy, dressed
in his striped apron and all, came out of a side-road on his
bicycle and neatly slid in between two of these monsters and
pedalled along at their pace, completely oblivious of them. As
if it was the most normal thing in the world to have such

traffic on the roads. By now, I suppose it is. Travelling here in that convoy I had a sudden picture of the whole war effort building up to a climax and concentrating on this area. Goods trains coming from the north with supplies. Factory workers shifting shells on a production line. Girls in prefabricated sheds packing parachutes under No Smoking notices. Soldiers loading equipment into landing-craft or supervising the movement of artillery by crane along the docks. GIs marching down the quayside to swell the ranks. Everywhere an endless and incessant activity. Bees in a hive, making a deadly honey.

Getting into the town, it was the same story. Already it was packed with servicemen. What civilians we saw seemed indifferent to yet another convoy moving through, although a group of workmen waved at our lorry and shouted, 'Best of luck! You'll be there!' 'Where?' I wanted to know. 'Where indeed?' said Arthur cryptically. Jack went on smoking and said nothing.

And so, we arrived here, in mid-afternoon. It is a sort of camp under canvas, but it's officially a Marshalling Area. My first sight of it was about as off-putting as it could have been. An enormous area of forest and heathland has been cordoned off with a barbed-wire fence. Machine-gun posts are dotted along it at intervals. They aren't manned yet, because we're the first arrivals. But it isn't a prospect calculated to raise morale. In fact it looks like the drawings of German POW camps I've seen in the newspaper. Arthur said the machine-guns were going to be directed outwards to stop civilians from rushing to volunteer for the invasion. Somehow I don't think so.

We were allocated bell-tents, and told to parade at 1600 hours in a place laughably called the Hotel Service Area, in front of the Dining Hall. Meanwhile we had to collect our palliasses and blankets from the Stores nearby and this took the best part of an hour, what with the usual queue and signing for the bedding, as we have to sign for everything in the Army including our lives. The parade at 1600 hours was a bit of an anticlimax. We'd been expecting to be told that the Second Front had opened or at least that it was under way. Instead a Captain with a pale face and a long ginger moustache told us that we had arrived at our destination. As if it wasn't obvious. And that we were to stand by for further instructions 'in the next few days'. Then we were dismissed, to trail back to the NAAFI or to our tents and contemplate the chance of another long delay doing nothing in surroundings much less comfortable than before. Arthur's been going on about it. Even Jack is a bit grumpy. I'm the only one not to care about the comfort or the surroundings. For me there is only one difference between this Marshalling Area and the other Camp. That's the difference between black and white. Life and death. Happiness and misery. Here I will not be able to see Janey. I may never see her again. A great way to celebrate my twenty-first birthday.

18 MAY

It was a warm evening. We both knew it might be for the last time. She was wearing a green jumper and a pleated grey skirt. She was shy and a bit nervous, like she was that first evening. I suppose it's natural to be awed by the unknownness of all the time that came before and all the time that's to come after. It was a warm evening. I've said that. We rode away from the village and people. She sitting side-saddle, light as a feather, worrying about laddering her only nylon stockings. She was wearing her mother's perfume. She felt warm and soft and deliciously close to me. One arm around me, hugging me tight.

There was a long hill. We walked up, not saying very much, talking about trivial things. Anything but the War.

She'd once or twice met the old woman who owned the big house I was quartered in. Usually she'd send her servants to the shop, but sometimes she'd sweep in through the clanging door, furling her parasol she always carried come rain or shine. A second copy of *The Times* it might be, if one of her society friends had died, or a box of the special mint chocolate which they stocked just for her. Years ago, when she was hardly big enough to look over the counter, the old woman had given her one of these chocolates. Leaning over and popping it into her mouth like a pill. It was said in the village that she wasn't coming back from Scotland. She couldn't bear to see what had been done to the house she loved. She was making arrangements through her agent to sell it to an American University.

We got to the top of the hill and turned off the road to walk hand in hand through the beech wood to a place we knew from before. What might be, and what might have been. To own a small house and a garden with a vegetable plot and no air-raid shelter. To go to work in the morning and work at our own pace, and come home in the evening through a street bright with lamplight and the light from windows. To have children for whom the roar of aeroplanes would mean travel to distant places. Not explosions, choking flames and sudden death.

The breeze was so slight it hardly ruffled the new green leaves. She bent down to pick mushrooms without leaving go of my hand. She held them out 'Let's eat them for dinner,' she suggested. They were white and succulent-looking like horse-mushrooms, but I remembered enough from working on the farm to know that woodland mushrooms in spring are best avoided. Sure enough, they had the double rings of the Death Cap and I made her throw them away, spit on her fingers and rub them on my sleeve. 'What am I going to do without you?' she said, laughing. 'Find somebody else,' I said without thinking. We walked on for a bit in silence. 'I've

95

been reading *The Times'* agony columns,' she said at last. 'Did you know that people are still putting in advertisements for salmon fishing and hiring exempt nannies and valets? Doesn't it make you sick?'

So we got to talking about what we are fighting for. I told her about standing in the library of the great house and looking out over the headland and thinking about traditions. Janey is so confident that things are going to start over again when all this is finished. I wanted so much to be there and starting them with her. Without fear or hopelessness or this terrible uncertainty.

We came to the place we had been before. A sudden opening in the beech wood and the ground sloping down greenly and speedwell and campion growing freely out of the shadow of the trees. A faint muffled growl came up from the roadway down below. If I stood on tiptoe or she sat on my shoulders we could see the sea, never many miles away. But I was going to see too much of that soon enough. I didn't want to stand on tiptoe today. I wanted to lie on the grass and she with me, in the last of the afternoon sun.

She put her arms behind her head and watched me as I knelt on the grass beside her, not knowing what to say. 'I'm going away tomorrow,' I started. 'I know,' she said. 'I love you,' I said. 'I know that, too.' So I lay close to her and kissed her, putting my hand underneath her green jumper to find, as I expected, that she was naked beneath it. She unfastened her hair and shook it out, long, dark and lovely.

There was no other sound but us. I unzipped her skirt. She tried to stop me, but only, as I discovered, because she didn't trust her precious nylon stockings to my clumsy fingers. Her legs were white and perfect. Her whole body as beautiful as I'd imagined it under that old-fashioned summery-patterned dress. The red flush had come back to her cheeks and she said in a whisper. 'Oh! Tom, Tom, I love you, please don't go away!' I didn't.

Afterwards we lay quietly to let the world which had gathered up in us float back to normal. There were voices above us. Two planes roared overhead and circled out over the sea. Traffic started up again on the road below. A mild wind which hadn't been there before blew strands of dark hair across her face. The voices came closer. A man's and a woman's, until they were almost above us. One said, 'I love you.' The other said, 'I love you too.' We finished dressing quietly and went away from that place without being seen, through the spring flowers into the dark of the beech wood. It was all we had left to say to each other.

19 MAY

I'm lonely here. There's nothing for us to do . . .

23 MAY

Another couple of platoons from the 1st Battalion South Lancs. arrived last night. The place is bursting at the seams. Security clamp-down on everything. News is coming through that the British, with the help of tremendous air support, have launched an offensive from the Anzio beach-head.

24 MAY

Here we go. Woke up early and looked out to see guards patrolling the barbed-wire perimeter and the helmets of sentries in the machine-gun posts. Rats in a trap. The Tannoy spluttered into life and told us all to parade in the Hotel Service Area at 0900 hours. We waited at attention for about ten minutes and then the Company Commander walked over from the Admin Tent. He'd cut his chin while shaving and had a ridiculous little piece of white fluff on it which he fingered all the time he was talking to us. It was one of those occasions where you remember everything very vividly afterwards. The place I was standing (centre rear behind a squat soldier called Andrews with two red pimples on the back of his neck), and the words spoken to us: 'You won't be doing any work. If you're wise you'll take advantage of all the rest you can get. Sorry about the tight security. It means no wireless sets, newspapers or telephoning, and I'm afraid none of your letters will get posted until afterwards. I'm sure all of you realize the importance of what lies ahead. That's all for now . . .' and, having pronounced our prison sentence, he strolled off still fingering his chin, while the rest of us stood to attention until he was out of sight.

No telephone calls? There haven't been any allowed since mid-April so that's no hardship. And we can still get letters. That's good. But none of *our* letters will get posted. I've been writing to Janey every day. When they don't come, will she think I'm dead?

25 MAY

Jancy came to see me last night. It was late and most of us were in bed. Jack was cleaning his boots. Arthur and Andrews, the man with pimples, were playing poker by the light of the paraffin lamp. She came in through the flap of the bell-tent, quite naturally, as if she hadn't had to ask the way, and sat down on my palliasse beside me. Nobody looked up. I don't think any of them noticed. I wanted to reach out and take her in my arms but I was rooted to the spot. She was very close to me and a very long way away.

She said, 'I thought you were meeting me tonight?' I

answered her mechanically, 'I was called away.' 'Why?' 'To fight the War.' 'Couldn't you have told me?' 'There was no time.' 'So you left me?' 'There was no choice.' In her eyes there were tears. She put out her hand to touch my face, but drew it away and let it fall in her lap. 'Are you coming back?' she said sadly. 'I don't know.' 'Am I going to wait for you?' 'I don't know.' She stood up, still so close, so close. 'I do though. Goodbye, Tom.' I made a great effort to move my limbs. I called out to her, in a whisper, 'Please! Don't go!' And I found I could move. The spell was broken. I could get off the bed, I could go to her, embrace her, never let her go.

But she was no longer there. The tent was dark. Arthur and Jack had long since gone to sleep. I stumbled out of bed and opened the tent-flap. The field was still and the moonlight hung glittering on the barbed wire. Already there are people for whom I don't exist.

26 MAY

Very intricate operation, waterproofing. Takes your mind off things. This morning Sergeant Johnson assembled us under the camouflage nets in the vehicle hides along the road from what's called the Sleeping Area. Apparently all vehicles have to be able to be driven in four feet of water, with the driver up to his waist or chest in water and his foot hard down on the accelerator. If LCTs are brought to a halt further from the beach, they might have to cope with even deeper water. This means that the entire vehicle has to be sealed. We were set to work with a kind of sticky putty, to seal every crevice through which water could reach the engine or the interior. After three hours of concentrated effort, our squad had succeeded in sealing about twenty vehicles. We broke for a sandwich lunch, feeling pleased that at long last we had done something constructive towards the war effort. After lunch we were instructed to remove all the sealer we had put on, and start again with a slightly different sort of putty. I have spent days of my life taking a simple rifle apart and putting it together again, but this was ridiculous. It took over an hour to get the first sealer off, and another couple of hours to waterproof the engines again. It turned out that the first time we'd been issued with 'practice' putty, and only now were we being entrusted with the real stuff. Over the next few days all the vehicles in these hides are having to be waterproofed, and the platoon is being put on a roster for daily inspections to ensure that the sealing hasn't deteriorated.

In the late afternoon we were taken into the Briefing Area, specially cordoned off from the rest of the Marshalling Area with ropes and guards. In the middle are three or four huts. The one we were taken into had benches facing a blackboard, like a country schoolroom. A lieutenant came in, very formal, to deliver us a lecture about Falling into the Hands of the Enemy. 'The first thing I must tell you,' he began, 'is that you must at all times attempt to avoid falling into the hands of the enemy.' Officers divide into those who treat you like morons and those who treat you like human beings – it was obvious where this one stood. 'Give your interrogator your name, rank and number,' he said, 'and no further details, especially no details about your battalion and regiment.'

He set us question-and-answer sessions 'in the interests of verisimilitude', one of us pretending to be a prisoner of war and the other a nasty Hun. The first round. Jack was the German interrogator and Arthur was his prisoner. Jack came over, dragged Arthur on to the floor and put his boot in him. 'There's no need for that,' protested the lieutenant. 'I was just trying for verisimilitude, sir,' said Jack. He glared down at Arthur, who promptly without being asked said, '24739 Arthur Cobbing, Private.' 'Will you tell me your regiment?' asked Jack in a heavy Hunnish voice. 'Never,' said Arthur. 'What if

100

I say I am going to tear your balls off?' 'Second battalion, East Yorks.' said Arthur.

At that point the lecture adjourned and we went off to the NAAFI for a drink.

28 MAY

It's amazing what creatures of habit and obedience we become in the Army. I'd have thought that being cut off from all external contact would have made me fascinated and curious about what's going on in the outside world. Instead I couldn't care less. In fact it's a relief not to have to bother with anything outside my own needs and duties here. If I didn't miss Janey so much, I'd be perfectly happy in this enclosed, secret space. It's like being back in the womb. I can quite easily understand how soldiers come to obey every order they're given, even if it's to shoot innocent people. The Army is mother and lawgiver rolled into one, and you can't disobey both at once. The only things that filter through the screen are the sort of jokes and idioms that no barrier keeps out. The latest joke phrase is 'Holidays at Home This Year.'

The weather is still warm and close. With eight of us in the bell-tent it's difficult to sleep, or sleep soundly. Maybe that's why I've been having such vivid dreams. Sometimes I'm at home. I've been called up and I know I have to be at the Camp on time. I leave home, running, with my suitcase. The Camp is only just down the street, but there is a sniper at the window, and I have to weave to avoid the mines in the road. The Sergeant is standing waiting for me at the Camp gates with a stop-watch, and just as I think how like the White Rabbit he looks, I find myself falling, falling down a deep bottomless hole.

I am getting used to that one. But I shall never get used to the landing-craft one. Even asleep and dreaming, I recognize it with a sinking feeling as a premonition of death. Sometimes I just get flashes of it. The ramp falling, say, or the boots plunging through water, or the rifle flung away in agony. But at once I know it for what it is, and wake up trembling and sweating, and praying for dreamless sleep.

In the mornings it is fine, especially if I've been spared the landing-craft the night before. Yesterday we staged our own circus version of a Commando exercise, tying a rope up high between two trees and tossing people up from a blanket to see who could grab the rope and hold on long enough to get to one of the trees and down that way. There are boxing matches, too. One poor bloke got so badly punched, the MO diagnosed a broken jaw and had him taken off the assault, although he still isn't allowed out of the Marshalling Area. What with that and film shows (the usual Charlie Chaplins I've seen a hundred times before), and housey-housey and equipment inspections, and reading (I'm on to *The Pickwick Papers* now, and not finding it very funny) and drinking lemonade in the NAAFI when the beer runs out, nobody can say there isn't plenty to write home about. In fact I've written five letters to Janey since Tuesday. I've packed them in the bottom of my kitbag. I'll send them to her after. Or someone else can.

30 MAY

It gets more macabre every day, these preparations. The Army is getting ready to sacrifice us, like vestal virgins. All that's missing are the drums and the war-dance. First thing this morning, it was the queue for haircuts. We're going to foreign parts and His Majesty's Armed Forces may be attacked by lice. So we had to be given short haircuts, and came out of the tent looking like bullet-headed thugs, indistinguishable from GIs. It's a bit demoralizing, like being shaved before an operation.

Like convicts then we shuffled forward to the next marquee and were given Description on Attestation cards to fill in. Army number, surname, Christian name, date of birth, religious denomination and next of kin. There was a blank space for fingerprints – 'Left Thumb', 'Right Thumb', and an ink-pad on the table. Apparently this has been started by the Americans. I pressed down my thumbs and looked at the rings spiralling out neatly from the whorl at the centre. I suppose these are for identifying me if there's nothing else recognizable. But it seems a waste of labour all the same. With charred corpses lying about, and bodies dismembered by mines and shrapnel, what medical orderly in the heat of battle is going to hold up the broken limbs, delicately dust the fingers with powder and transfer their imprint to paper? They'll do what they did in the First World War. Bury what they can find and inscribe above the remains a selection of missing persons believed to have been in the vicinity.

The tabulating went on. The next queue was for the photographer's booth. I held my army number and stood to attention while the flashlight went off. 'Next please,' said a voice from somewhere. 'If I'm killed,' I said, 'they've already got a photograph!' A plump bespectacled face peered round the curtain. 'It's for Army records, Private Beddows,' it said severely. There was a queue, so I didn't argue. It isn't standard Army practice, I heard this evening, it's just that the Company Commander is a keen photographer.

What next? There were queues of soldiers stretching all over the Admin Area by now, in and out of marquees, like a life-size game of snakes and ladders. By the time I got my anti-louse wear I was getting depressed and morbid. The last instruction of the day didn't help. It's been to fill in a will-form, B2090 if it's complicated, or B2089 if it's all going to one person. After the photograph I didn't have the heart to ask what the point of it was, but Arthur did, in front of me. 'What do you think?' said the clerk wearily. Arthur didn't ask a second time.

I chose 2089 since it was less trouble, filled in name, rank, number and regiment, and Hereby revoked all Wills heretofore made by me at any time and declared this to be my last Will and Testament. I appointed Dad my executor, for what it's worth. After payment of my just Debts and Funeral Expenses, I give all my Estates and Effects, and everything that I can give or dispose of to him and Mum. Except for any lice, which I leave to the Army. Signed this thirtieth day of May, 1944.

A big deal. My books, a child's stamp-collection, a dozen 78s, my bicycle, a decent suit I'd bought before the call-up papers came, a framed engraving of Halifax in 1850 I bought in a junk shop, and a photograph which was Dad's anyway before he got a new one. Since I couldn't write a covering letter home, I had to scrawl a message on the bottom of the form in small handwriting. 'Please sell my goods up to value £7 and buy gold ring (small size) from jewellers and send to Miss Janey Cribbins, 11 High Street, Tyneham, Dorset, with my love.'

31 MAY

French francs given out. That settles where we're going. We lined up in front of two tables in the open air. Wads of paper money were stacked up, and we were each handed a small wad and a new pay book at the same time. At the next table our money was counted and our names checked against a register. We were advised to hand all our English money to the Adjutant's orderly 'for safe keeping'. Since we couldn't very well take it to France with us, it seems a sensible thing to do. Nobody knows whether the French will accept this money, and for a couple of people in the tent it doesn't make much difference, since Arthur has already won most of it off them at poker and dice. It makes a change from playing with matchsticks.

Security is amazingly tight. After this afternoon's map-briefing, I still don't have a clue what part of France we're heading for. It could be anywhere between Calais and Marseilles. A very large-scale plan of the coastal assault area was laid out on a table and held down with ammo boxes. The briefing officers pointed out the landmarks (the lieutenant who'd lectured us used an ornamental dagger). The villages were given the names of Scottish towns, like Helensburgh, and the shoreline has been given the name Red Beach. The entire area has been code-named Hungary. Apparently someone thought he knew where it was, because the briefing was stopped while a signal officer reminded us that we had all been sworn to secrecy and must not talk about possible locations even among ourselves. But the whole thing couldn't have been more than a mile of coastline. I don't see how anyone could have known.

The landmarks have been plotted in incredible detail. Every house and lane is marked. There are symbols to represent pillboxes, minefields, road-blocks and battery positions. Jack asked how we were to know whether the beach was firm enough to fight over. He was told that the battalion officer had been shown an aerial photograph of the section on which a horse and cart could be seen going across the sand.

Our unit was taken into a briefing hut then and we were shown snapshots of the beach, taken seven hundred yards from the shore. Directly ahead of us will be a group of houses, which will be shelled before the assault by bombardment ships, but which may still harbour snipers who have to be winkled out. On the right, beyond the houses, the ground rises slowly towards a clump of bushes, falls sharply, and rises again to a high bluff which projects out slightly and commands the village. We were told that the clump of bushes hid a pillbox, that the farmhouse, of which the pictures showed us the roof and upper storey, contained another German gun position, and that there was a concrete artillery emplacement on the bluff which would be our second objective if it hadn't already been knocked out by our naval guns. What the Briefing Officer didn't need to point out was that if this artillery emplacement wasn't knocked out either by the Navy or our first assault wave, Red Beach was going to be red in more than name. I didn't see how the Krauts could help but blow us out of the water in any case, but then the Briefing Officer said, 'The first assault will be going in at, or shortly before, dawn, so it is important to familiarize yourselves with the shapes of these landmarks in the semi-darkness.' Thank the Lord for small mercies.

I must stop now. Arthur and I have been planning all day to try and find a way out of this compound tonight, for a last fling of freedom before the drawbridge goes up and the portcullis comes down. Arthur's even kept some English money back in case he finds a nice girl to give parting comfort to a heroic soldier boy. He's just come over to tell me he's found a possible way out through the barbed wire behind the ammo dump. It's a part of the compound that's so well camouflaged against the Germans that our own guard patrols get confused. There are still enough people around for it not to look suspicious. Cape and walking shoes, and hope we're lucky.

1 JUNE

Of course this had to be the one place in England where it rained most of Wednesday night. There were clouds and a chill in the air when we slipped under the wire, but nothing serious. Then it started to drizzle. What we'd forgotten was that the town would be swarming with American military police keeping an eye out for anybody in uniform. They stayed mostly down by the quayside. For the first time I got a glimpse of the sheer dimensions of what we're entered upon. Before the war it must have been a peaceful harbour, with a small fishing fleet, beach huts for swimming and pleasure boats taking holiday-makers on excursions. The sea wall had been dismantled for a stretch of a hundred yards or more and square sections of black rubberized tiles, looking like slabs of chocolate, ran from the promenade to the water's edge. Work-men were still busily extending it, hauling slabs of tiling off trolleys and fitting them into place. These were the 'hards' I'd heard about. Landing-craft and troop-carriers of all shapes and sizes lay close inshore. At the far end of the jetty a new LCT was being launched. It slid forward, hung balanced for a moment, then plunged down into the water almost vertically, with an enormous splash which nearly swamped a little DUKW* bobbing past towards the beach.

Watching these vast and complicated preparations I wondered for the first time what would happen if it didn't come off. If the invasion was a failure and we were thrown back into the sea. It didn't seem possible. And yet we all know what happened at Dieppe. I suppose I've never thought of it before because I've never thought it was going to matter to me. Like a guest at a party who's unavoidably called away before it gets properly started. But I don't think the others either have given much thought to success or failure. The operation is too big for that. Our individual bit helps the squad, which helps the platoon, which helps the Company . . . and what's one Company in terms of battle? Chicken-feed. One of Rommel's Panzer divisions could wipe us out in an afternoon and hardly notice it. Thinking this, Arthur and I walked into the town centre. We didn't look too conspicuous in our capes. But what good-time girls there are to be found in a well-bred resort like this had packed up and gone home to their aunties. We mooched around disconsolately for a while, looking at the mannequins in shop windows. 'If I could bore a hole in that I'd take it home with me,' said Arthur, pressing against the glass. Then the rain really set in.

* An amphibious vehicle.

107

We didn't dare go into a pub for fear of being picked up – by the MPs, I mean. So we ran down the street and took shelter in the first doorway we came to. I wasn't going to walk through that lot. So much for the seaside.

Arthur heard it first. A strange mewling sound and the faint tinkling of a piano. He tried the door. It opened and the noise resolved itself into the sound of a child singing. A short passage led to some circular stone steps. At the top, a maroon curtain. We pushed past and found ourselves to our amazement in the Circle of a music hall. All the seats were empty, but the place was not deserted. On the stage below stood a tiny girl in a white party dress. She was singing all by herself to the empty auditorium in a shrill, faltering voice – 'Let him go, let him tarry, let him sink or let him swim, he doesn't care for me and I don't care for him.' It was an eerie sight, the little girl and the great dark auditorium, and we went to the rail for a closer look. In the orchestra pit were an old man playing an upright piano, and a buxom woman, clearly the child's mother, conducting and singing along at the same time.

She saw us and waved at us to sit down, then redoubled her efforts to get the poor child to sing louder. 'You've got an audience now!' she yelled, putting her daughter through her paces for some talent competition, I suppose, and the girl stood there unhappily with her hands clutched behind her back singing. 'He can go and get another that I hope he will enjoy, for I'm going to marry a far nicer boy.' It's a song you hear everywhere these days, and I hate it, as do all the men I know who are going off to war and leaving their girls behind. The song came to an end, and the woman's voice floated up, chirpy and relentless, 'Sing it again, Susannah, right through, once more for the soldiers.' '*Please*, Mummy!' pleaded the girl miserably. I thought she was going to offer to do her Shirley Temple tap-dance instead. The old man took it from the beginning. *Let him go* ... sang the child. *Let him sink* ...

Arthur and I made our way back to the exit, and the woman's voice came up from below: 'Don't go, Tommies. Tommies, please don't go!'

Outside, the rain had steadied to a drizzle. We walked back in silence.

SAME AFTERNOON

I've done nothing all day except write in this diary, read a few more pages of *The Pickwick Papers* and go and eat in the Mess Area. I got the impression that things were accelerating, but they seem to have slowed down again. All they are doing is feeding us up like pigs for the slaughter. Jack's pretty depressed by it. 'Cannon fodder, that's what we are,' he says. 'Die of boredom, die in battle, what's the difference?' I know how he feels. We're all a bit demoralized by these days of waiting.

Arthur hit on a brilliant idea this morning, as if last night's escape wasn't enough. He went to see the Company Adjutant and asked him if they gave out compassionate leave if there'd been a death in the family. The Adjutant, a cautious old bugger, said, 'Yes, depending on the circumstances.' So Arthur said, 'Well, there hasn't been a death in my family yet, but there's going to be one *very soon*. I request leave to go home and console my parents!' Jack told me this, just now. It's the first time I've seen him laugh for days. Apparently the Adjutant wasn't so amused. He sent Arthur with a sealed note to the MO. The MO read it and asked Arthur what had happened. Then he said, 'The Adjutant's note recommends a strong dose of salts. I'll let you off this time, but if I see you in here again, I'll break both your legs and make you walk to France.'

Oh yes, and my birthday mail arrived, or as much of it as I'm likely to see. Jack and Arthur were both in the tent and watched while I opened it. Arthur hasn't heard from his bird recently, and Jack, who never talks about his home life, hasn't had a letter that I've seen all the time he's been here. There were a couple of birthday cards from aunts and uncles, the usual kind of thing they send every year and would send to Hell if they knew the right address. Then there was a dirty postcard from Bob. It read – 'Hope you are Living it Up before the Big Day. I'm getting my fair WAAC daily. All the best, Bob.' Then there was an unsigned card with a message written in green ink: 'We'll meet again. Don't know where. Don't know when. But I know we'll meet again some happy day.' I couldn't read the postmark to tell where it came from. But who else could it be?

Finally there was a bulky letter from home. I opened it, and out fell a key made of cardboard and silver foil, the silliest thing I've ever seen. Arthur wanted to know what it was for. 'It's a funny sort of birthday present,' he said. I explained rather lamely that it was the custom in my family. Key of the door, coming of age, that sort of thing. They both seemed amazed. 'You just twenty-one?' asked Jack, as if he thought I was in my thirties. 'Happy birthday, kid,' said Arthur, doing his Bogart drawl, 'and plenty more of them.'

I'm really lucky that they're both going through this thing with me.

The letter from home is full of the usual nonsense. Mum has heard that there's been an outbreak of lice in some army camps and asks if I'm washing my hair every day. Tina has had puppies unexpectedly. Probably the piebald mongrel down the street that's had his eye on her for years. Dad has had promotion into a slightly higher pay bracket. He adds a scrawl at the bottom of Mum's neat handwriting, and asks, 'Have you had any time for reading? I never did.' I'm sure he's said that to me before. Good old Dad and his ideas of self-education. Pulling me up by my bootstrings.

The bulky object in the envelope was a fine fountain-pen,

which must have cost them a lot of money. I took it out and showed it to Jack, who was impressed, and suddenly I felt a great fondness and love for Mum and Dad which I haven't felt in a long time. Jack asked, humbly as if it was a great favour, if he could have a look at my birthday cards. I left him there with them and went to the NAAFI to buy some ink to write back home. With pen and paper I walked out to the small piece of woodland, near the Vehicle Hides, that is enclosed within the Camp perimeter. I sat down with my back against a tree. There was nobody in sight, and no noise apart from the gurgle of a wood-pigeon. Perhaps because of my love for them, I suddenly felt a great sadness and sense of responsibility as well. I know that this letter, like the ones I've written to Janey, won't get posted until after we're in France. But I've held back too long from telling them my conviction that I'm going to get killed in this War. There have been plenty of reasons for it. I didn't want to distress them unnecessarily. I half-thought it was a superstition which would come and go. But I know better now. It is a solid thing I dread. It has grown with me like an animal waiting to turn on me when the moment comes. It is time to be honest about it.

2 JUNE

As I write, I am resting this diary on the groundsheet beside my bed. When I hear footsteps, I slip it under the blanket and pretend to be reading. If I am found out, this and the other diaries will be taken away. For all I know, I will be court-martialled.

I've nothing else left. At morning parade, we were addressed by the Company Commander. He said that as assault troops in the first wave, it was quite possible that if captured we would not be given the treatment accorded to prisoners of war. It was therefore necessary to dispose of all documents, including personal letters and papers, that might reveal more than our name, rank and number. We had a choice between burning them or packing them up and sending them to our next of kin. On the invasion we would be allowed to carry nothing except our Pay Book, Part One and Bible.

We were told to assemble at 1100 hours. We were made to parade with kitbags, so that nothing could be hidden. I'd ripped a hole in my palliasse with Jack's clasp-knife and stuffed these diaries inside. Everything else I was carrying. By platoon we were marched to the Waterproofing Area. The tanks etc. had been taken down to the quayside earlier today and the camouflage nets had been dismantled. In the open space, a bonfire was burning. We were told to stand in a circle and unpack our kitbags. When our belongings were lying on the grass in front of us, the Adjutant's clerk came round with a square of brown paper for each of us. What we didn't pack up to be sent home had to be thrown on the fire.

I don't know how long I stood there. Men made journeys to and from the fire with letters and mementoes. I couldn't send home my letters to Janey. Mum would be sure to read them. Nor did I want her to get my last letter in a bundle wrapped up with odds and ends. Better to get rid of everything. To go out the way I came in. The old feeling came over me, the same one I first had at training camp, climbing down that hill which grew steeper and rockier before the sudden drop . . . the falling . . . I thought, you've got nothing to lose. I walked forward to the fire. Letters were burning on it, many of them love letters which could not be replaced or repeated, the words blackening, the ashes blowing on the wind. I threw in Janey's birthday card and watched it burn. Don't know where, don't know when. I threw in my letters to Janey, all that she might have known of me in these final days. Lastly I threw on the flames my letter home.

I don't know if that was a wise thing. In case this diary

survives me, I shall write down my letter as well as I can remember it. Whoever else reads here, Mum and Dad, this letter was for you alone.

Army Post Office, England.

Dearest Mum and Dad

Thank you very much for your letter, and the presents, which have just arrived. My fountain-pen works very well, as you can see. We're very cut off here, as you can see from the address. I don't know where we are exactly, and it was so nice to hear from you. You don't have to worry about me. We're eating very well in this camp. Although the beds are hard, I'm getting plenty of sleep. We all think Monty's Moon can't be far off. It's like being part of a machine which gets bigger and bigger, while we grow smaller and smaller until there's nothing left.

I wish I had some news. Yesterday I saw a fox on the other side of the barbed wire. We have been having lots of lectures and briefings which I can't tell you about. The Camp cinema has been showing old comedies, but when we could still go out, I went to see *This Happy Breed* with Celia Johnson in it. I thought it was terrific at the time, but I can't remember much about it now. It seems so distant. Everything outside the Army and my mates here has faded away. I must have done more travelling in the last two weeks even than when I went to France on that school holiday, but I couldn't tell you where we are or where we've come from. All we seem to do is sit in trucks and barracks, waiting for our bit of the war to start.

At any other time your news of Dad's promotion would have left me unable to think of anything else. But now it just seems part of the War like everything else. Tina too. I was going to ask you to keep one of the puppies, but I don't think there is much point. The fact is, I don't think I shall live here to see the end of this War. It sounds silly, but this war has killed so many people already, I'm just going to be another one. Of that I'm sure. I can feel it, the way you feel it when you are going to get a cold.

I didn't know whether to tell you. I thought you shouldn't get one of those official letters without knowing what was inside it. Please be brave. I shall be all right. I'm not frightened.

3 JUNE

I think that barbed-wire compound must have been putting everybody's nerves on edge. Now we're on board, everything has relaxed a bit, including security. I'm sitting writing this on deck, leaning against a ship's derrick, and no one's paid me the least attention. In fact I think I might spend the night out here. Down in the hold the bunks are six deep, it's worse than the bell-tent. Up here I've got the sea air and a good view back to the quayside.

For the second day running, the Camp Commander took the morning parade. This time it was to give us the news we'd been waiting for. As usual, instead of giving it to us simply, he talked in a weird kind of officer-language that needed translating as he went along. 'Well, men, I'm glad to tell you our bit of the fun's about to start. We'll be embarking today, and in no time at all we'll have the chance to take a swipe at Jerry in his own backyard. I know that's what you've been waiting for, and, by George, we're ready for the off. We're going in on a sticky wicket. You know that. But man for man, Jerry's no match for us, and we'll lick him into the ground. Just bear in mind – it won't be long now.'

We all cheered, as if we were about to set out on a works' holiday. The Chaplain got on his hind legs to give us a few words of heavenly comfort, and we cheered him too. We must be bloody mad. We were split into our sections after that. The sergeants took charge, and the holiday was over. We were issued with various sizes of rubberized bags, in which everything had to be packed, including signal equipment. Everything else had to be carried on and around us. On our backs: big and small packs, blanket, greatcoat, groundsheet and gas cape. On our chests: the gas mask. Around our waists: laden ammunition pouches, water-bottle, bayonet and mug. Over our shoulders: helmet, rifle and kitbag. In this Michelin Man outfit, the idea of actually fighting is plain ridiculous. It was all we could do to walk.

At 1500 hours, rank upon rank, we staggered out of the compound, leaving the barbed wire behind us for good and all. Arthur, who is fond of quoting Churchill at the worst possible moment, said, 'This is not the end. It is not even the beginning of the end. But it is, perhaps, the end of the beginning.' Johnson told him to shut up. Down at the quayside we were told to fall out and sit on crates along the outside wall of what used to be the ticket-office for the pleasure-boat excursions round the bay. Tea-urns came round, and we spent the next ninety minutes drinking what might well be our last cups of tea. That's what we reckon anyway. Most of the voices I heard on the quayside had American (or Canadian) accents, and the only LCTs I could see in harbour had US painted on the side in big white letters.

The Tannoy has just broadcast an order to assemble on the main deck. I'd better get this out of sight.

4 JUNE

I didn't sleep much last night. Early this morning, just as dawn was breaking, I came up on deck to see if the coast of France was in sight. The weather had taken a turn for the worse. Visibility was down to a few hundred yards. All I could see was the transport ship along from us in the convoy, flashing signals through the gloom. Something strange was going on. I couldn't make out what it was at first. Then I realized that our engines had stopped. We were hove to. I made my way along the deck towards the bow. The rain was blowing across in squalls, and the heavy swell meant it was difficult to keep my balance. One of the US crewmen came past. I asked him what was happening. He said, 'It's been postponed.'

It took a little while to sink in. The great machine has sometimes been slow-moving but its wheels have always turned in the right direction. Now, all of a sudden, it's stopped completely. It is a bad sign. The sky had cleared somewhat and now I could see a shoreline behind us. But it wasn't France. It was the Isle of Wight. I didn't know that at the time, but I do now. It's still there, behind us. The small buoys strung out somewhere in front have lost their purpose. They were supposed to indicate the swift channel route to France.

All day we've stayed on board this LCT. Some units had to embark on the little tank-carrying ships, and they're the ones I feel really sorry for in this weather, what with the discomfort and the smell of petrol. Conditions on this American boat aren't good, but at least we have room to sleep, and plenty of food for those that can eat it. I'm one of the lucky ones. The only other time I've been to sea, on the cross-Channel ferry going to Boulogne, it was rougher than this and I wasn't seasick. I've felt fine today so long as I've stayed on deck. All I miss is a cup of tea to settle my stomach properly. The Americans have black coffee and cold water on tap in the galley, but I've never much fancied black coffee.

Down in the hold, things aren't too good. The news about the postponement came over the Tannoy. Since then we've been in limbo. We can't sail and we can't go back to shore.

Arthur found a poker group and that went all right for a

while. I joined in, about midday. When our French money ran out (or ran into Arthur's pocket) we gambled for pints of French lager, payable when we get to Paris. To keep us alert we were given two or three rehearsals of action stations' drill. The first time, nobody knew that it wasn't the real thing. The alarm bell sounded six short rings. The sailors who were with us raced upstairs to their posts through the hatches, which were then battened down. We had to stand at or near our bunks, with life-jackets inflated. At first I couldn't inflate mine, no matter what bits of rubber I pulled or blew through. I had a horrifying vision of the ship sinking, and me with it, while every other man on board rose safely to the surface like bubbles in a bottle. I got mine to inflate eventually. But a number of people were still tugging desperately at their bits of string and rubber when a senior US naval officer came down to inspect us and we knew it was simply a practice.

Other than that, there's been nothing to do but sleep and eat and talk and look at the sea. The best story going around is about Henderson, whom I remember vaguely as a sandy-haired Geordie with freckles. Apparently he deserted from his regiment last year because he missed his girlfriend so much. He went back to live with her happily in Newcastle, and gave the Army the slip for *nine months*! Then, a fortnight ago, he walked into the compound as bold as brass, as if he'd never been away, and gave himself up to the guards. Apparently he's been saying that he didn't want to let his regiment down when the fighting started, so he bid a noble farewell to his lady and came south to offer his life for King and Country. More likely, says Jack, his bird got fed up with him and told him to sod off back to the Front. He's lucky not to have been shot. They tipped him straight into solitary and now they've packed him off with us on the first assault under armed guard! The lucky bugger is sleeping in the guardroom, which is a lot more comfortable than this hold. He'll probably get through the War without a scratch.

This afternoon, not before time, we were given our last issue of equipment. The British Army, at this moment of crisis, has begun worrying seriously about our laundry. We've been given specially impregnated anti-louse shirts and underwear, so that we can go for another twenty-four hours without washing. Mum would be pleased. We've also been issued with a condom to put over the muzzle of our rifle to keep the water out as we wade towards the beach. I can understand why they didn't issue *those* on shore.

And at the last minute, somebody has given thought to the conditions on board and issued us with seasickness precautions; chewing-gum, seasickness tablets (with the instructions 'To be taken One Hour before feeling Seasick') and three spew bags per man, as the final solution. The sight of these this afternoon was enough to send me up on deck.

SAME NIGHT

Sick for an hour. This evening the rain stopped and the wind grew lighter. An announcement came over the Tannoy. It was the Chaplain to say that a service would be held at 1930 hours on the port deck. Most of us didn't know what day it was.

But we went up on deck and found that the whole ship had come to the service. The American officers and crew were standing there, and so was Henderson with his guard. The Chaplain had put on his surplice and full vestments, which he'd never done before. He stood above us on a piece of engine casing, and while we listened in silence he read to us verses from the third chapter of St John, the same verses Dad has carried with him in the trenches in 1915: 'Marvel not that I said unto thee, Ye must be born again. The wind bloweth where it listeth, and thou hearest the sound thereof, but canst not tell where it cometh, and whither it goeth: so is every one that is born of the Spirit . . . For God so loved the world, that he gave his only begotten Son, that whosoever believeth in him should not perish, but have everlasting life . . . For everyone that doeth evil hateth the light, neither cometh to the light, lest his deeds should be reproved. But he that doeth truth cometh to the light, that his deeds may be made manifest, that they are wrought in God.'

To finish, we sang 'Abide with me, Fast falls the eventide'. I felt very good, and had a lump in my throat. Jack was twisting his cap in his hands. It must be that emotion is multiplied by the number of people who share it. When it was over, I could hear voices singing on the next ship along. I realized that all down the South Coast, from Weymouth to Dover and beyond, countless ships and landing-craft were at anchor, their fighting men singing the same hymn, under the same sunset. I stayed on deck after the Chaplain's blessing until everybody had dispersed, not wanting to lose such a feeling of fellowship. It was the first time since leaving Janey that I hadn't felt alone.

Now it's late. Down here in the hold the talking stopped long ago. We lie fully-dressed on our bunks, waiting for sleep to come, for some of us the last sleep we can be sure of waking from. Where we'll be when that awakening comes, nobody knows. Not us, not the officers, not the generals in charge. But I'm not going to go to sleep facing the wall, in case a torpedo comes through.

5 JUNE

It's 0530 in the morning. I've come up on deck. There's enough light to write by if I hold this diary close. For a long while I lay awake. Then I slept, and had the strangest dream about Janey. I was woken from that by the sound of people banging on windows and doors, to find it was the engines beating and the invasion under way. I couldn't have slept again, so I came on deck to write.

I was standing to attention, in full uniform, in the middle of the village hall. It was empty of furniture. There were no streamers, no band playing, no bar along the wall. Windows and a door, four walls, a floor and a ceiling. Everyone had gone off to the War. I was the last one left.

I stood there motionless. The door behind me opened and closed. Janey came and stood in front of me. She was wearing a white nurse's gown. She was barefoot, and her dark hair fell loosely around her shoulders. I felt nothing. I was a rock. I knew that I had said goodbye to her for the last time, and that this must be a Spirit summoned from the undiscovered country to tease my dreams. She advanced towards me and laid her hand upon my cheek. Her hand was cold. She smelled of air and light. She said to me softly, 'Shall I show you how we prepare the dead?'

She took off my helmet and laid it on the floor. She unbuttoned my battledress top and pulled it off me, and my vest also. Supporting me under my arms she laid me gently on the floor. My boots, gaiters and socks came off, and then my trousers. With a sharp knife she cut through the elastic of my pants. I lay on the floor naked, motionless and unspeaking. Kneeling beside me she leant over and with a kiss, sealed all the openings of my body, first shutting my eyes with her fingers. Lastly she kissed me on my mouth. Her lips were not cold. They were alive and warm and infinitely tender. This was no Spirit. I opened my eyes and it was Janey kneeling there. I was awake and she was there. 'Now bring me back,' I said.

Still looking at me with that sad and loving look, not taking her eyes off my face, she began slowly unbuttoning her nurse's gown. She took it by the sides and pulled it over her head. Under it she was wearing nothing. The soft light shone on her body and caught the movement of her breasts as she leaned over me, and I rose towards her with new life. Then came the banging on the windows, the hammering at the door. Janey was gone. The engines were turning. I was awake. I am awake. But I am not unprepared.

6 JUNE

0600 hours. The landing-craft has stopped moving forward. Grey light and a cold wind off the sea. The beach ahead. It's light enough now to see the landmarks they showed us, like it was in the photograph. The noise of the bombardment is incredible.

Thirty of us. Nothing to do but wait. There was a good breakfast for us at 0300, but nobody felt much like eating. I had seasickness pills and tinned apricots. Arthur had nothing at all. We assembled on deck at 0430 and were in the water in LCAs fifteen minutes later.

Before we left, we were given brown paper envelopes, with orders to dispose of the contents, once we'd studied them, in a bag provided for the purpose. Inside was a photocopy of the map we had been shown in our briefings. It was given the heading OVERLORD, an unfamiliar name to me. We were given a tot of rum and then we were off. Arthur said, 'I don't think I'm going to get through this.' I thought that was funny, considering. I put my arm round his shoulders and said, 'Don't worry, you'll be all right, we'll get you through.' And I meant it!

Even Jack is a little scared. Although he's hidden it. He told me why he never became an officer. He failed the initiative test! He was locked in a broken-down potting-shed and told to imagine he was a prisoner trying to escape. If he used that wall he'd be shot. If he climbed that fence he'd be electrocuted. If he trod here, there, anywhere, he'd be blown up by hidden mines. He didn't move a bloody inch! he said. If they hadn't come and let him out, he'd still have been in that potting-shed waiting to become an officer.

We've been told to keep our heads down below the gunwales. But the stink of fuel, oil, vomit and shit is bad enough without putting your nose in it. A dead soldier floated by, held up by his inflated life-jacket.

Arthur's being sick again. Jack's trying to cheer him up by reminding him of the names of all the women he's had since he's been in the Army (he's told us often enough). Belinda. Mabel. Alice, no, she was Jack's first.

Janey.

The bombardment is easing up. It can't be long now. I've checked my ammo. Keep a distance of six feet. Keep running. I'm not frightened. We're going in.

'We're going in.' That was the last thing Tom wrote. What happened to him? Was he alive or dead?

We contacted the Army Office, giving what information we could. Some time later we received a reply asking for further details and explaining that information about army personnel was normally supplied only to relatives and to persons who could give the necessary bona fides. *Meanwhile we returned to Mr Jackson for the full name of the previous owners of his house. With this information we again approached the local Council Office.*

There was a record of a Mrs M. Beddows living as a tenant in the Jacksons' house as late as 1961. Further searches uncovered the information that in the same year she had gone to a Home for elderly and infirm people, near Everton. The registrar at the Home confirmed that Mrs Margaret Beddows had come to stay in the Home in 1961, suffering from an unspecified form of bone disease. She had died in 1963. Her son, Mr Michael Beddows, had flown from Canada to supervise the funeral arrangements. The registrar had his address on file.

We cabled Mr Beddows in Canada. He sent us a telegram by return. It read simply, THOMAS BEDDOWS, 110–153

BAYEUX, NORMANDY. LETTER FOLLOWING. It arrived on the day we had scheduled to visit the Normandy beaches. Without telephoning or sending further cables, we travelled to Bayeux. From there we were directed to Roquentières.

Thomas Beddows was where we expected to find him. There was a gate in the brick wall. Inside, we walked past acres of well-cut grass. He was at Plot 110, Row G, Grave 153. A simple white headstone, inscribed 'Private Thomas Beddows 1923–1944'. We returned to England.

A packet of letters from Mr Michael Beddows was waiting for us in London. Besides his covering note, it contained a clipping from the News Chronicle *and three letters. With Mr Beddows' permission we publish them here.*

9 JUNE

Dear Sir and Madam,

You will by now have received the telegram and letter from the War Office telling you that your son was killed in action four days ago during the first Normandy landings. This is just a line to share my sympathy with you in your great loss. I was not in the landing-craft with him when he died, and as you know, the boat bringing his body back to the transport ship was mined and sank some way away from us. However, I conducted a burial service for him, and you may be sure that he will have his own memorial here, along with the other men who gave up their life for their country in this gallant assault.

I did not know Tom well, but I gather he was a fine, brave lad who will be sorely missed by us all. You have my deepest condolences.

Very sincerely yours,
T. E. Pennecuik, Chaplain

The next two letters, written from the Front by Jack and Arthur, are crumpled and stained, as if they had been read many times. They are undated, but from Arthur's descriptions of the fighting, we may assume that his letter was written less than a fortnight after Tom's death.

Dear Mr/Mrs Beddows

I want to say how sorry I am about Tom. He was a great chum of mine, and a good sort. I do not know if you heard what happened. We were in the L-craft coming in to shore and almost at the beach when Tom got his through the head. He was up to go and ping, like that, and it was all over. Arthur Cobbings and me came back when we saw it and held him between us but there was blood pumping out of his head and he died instantly so he wouldn't have felt pain. It was pretty hot round us, and we had to leave him there but I hope he got back to you safely. It's always worse for the ones back home and I am more sorry than I can say for you. He was a good sort.

Yrs respectfully,
Cpl. Jack Dyer

Dear Mr and Mrs Beddows

Tom was my best friend and I know how you must feel about him dying. We did training together right through and up to the training for the beach assault. Tom was always ready with a joke or to give a bloke a helping hand. We shall miss him very much as I am sure you do too. It is terrible this Front, we are fighting through a big town called Caen and this is the first moment I have had to sit down and write. Your son died in a flash, I hope we shall all be so lucky when the time comes, not to be gloomy but some of the cases you see round here you can be thankful that Tom got his cleanly. I must go now, so please accept all my sympathy.

Yours sincerely,
Arthur Cobbings

The cutting is from the News Chronicle *of 10 June 1944, a brief inch out of columns of obituaries. It reads:*

Thomas Beddows, Pvt. 8th Brigade, who gave his life for England in the furious fighting for the Normandy beaches, on the morning of 6 June. Thank you, dear, for having enriched our lives for 21 years. Mum, Dad, Michael and Tina.

The absence of the official telegram and War Office letter is explained in the covering note by Mr Michael Beddows. He writes:

I spent the war years in Canada and went on to University in Montreal in 1947. The year before that I came home to see Mother and Dad. It was not a happy house to stay in. Although Tom had been killed more than two years earlier, the whole place was filled with his memory. His photograph, showing him in uniform, was on the mantelpiece. My father would take it down and stare at it, or the tin model of the First World War soldier that stood beside it. He had been retired from the steelworks. His lungs, affected by gas in 1918, had been made worse by inhaling steel dust from the foundry. My mother tried to get him to work in the garden, or read, but he claimed he had no time for reading. He would spend whole days sitting in an armchair in the front room, brooding about Tom and my uncle, who had been killed beside him in Flanders. One day, shortly before he died, in a fit of bitterness he burned the official notifications of my brother's death and with them the letters Tom had sent home from Camp. My mother retrieved what she could. The enclosed letters she gave to me. The rest she hid away from my father in a place he would never find them, and kept their whereabouts secret from me as well . . .

With his letter, Mr Michael Beddows included a statistic our own research had uncovered. Within twenty-four hours, the Normandy beach-heads had been secured. At the cost of approximately 10,300 men killed or wounded, operation Overlord had achieved its first objectives.

DAZ 4 ZOE
Robert Swindells

'Here is a teenage novel with everything: love, loyalty, nail-biting suspense, some excellent writing, and a huge moral poser about where our Two Nations society will end. Set in a not-so-distant future world, the story is told through the alternate voices of the two young lovers. How the two teenagers meet and keep contact across the divide is nail-biting enough, but the story of their escape from the ties of their own communities and the security forces is brilliant, pulling few punches about the cost to others which their freedom must exact' – Aisling Foster, *Independent*.

TAKING THE FERRY HOME
Pam Conrad

Ali is instantly wildly jealous of Simone's beauty, wealth and confidence. But Simone is determined that the two should be friends for the summer. And so they become, for a seemingly perfect holiday of fun, friendship and romance. Simone even promises to help Ali get the gorgeous Brendan. But promises are hard for Simone.

In a dramatic climax to this gripping novel, Ali begins to realize that Simone's life isn't to be envied after all.

MADAME DOUBTFIRE
Anne Fine

Lydia, Christopher and Natalie Hilliard are used to domestic turmoil and have been torn between their warring parents ever since the divorce. But all that changes when their mother takes on a most unusual cleaning lady. Despite her extraordinary appearance, Madame Doubtfire turns out to be a talented and efficient housekeeper and, for a short time at least, the arrangement is a resounding success. But as the Hilliard children soon discover, there's more to Madame Doubtfire than domestic talents . . .

DOUBLE TAKE
June Oldham

When unemployed actress Olivia Quinn takes part in a small television news item about a missing girl, she triggers a series of dramatic events. Not only is she subjected to harassment, violence and prejudice, but events start to take on a disturbing similarity to those surrounding the missing girl's disappearance.

A SEAL UPON MY HEART
Pam Conrad

At the age of sixteen, Darcie suddenly becomes acutely aware of the lack of knowledge she has of her father. While her mother is away with her new husband, Darcie spends the summer playing detective to his whereabouts. She also finds friendship in the form of Roman, the seal-keeper at the zoo where she has a summer job. He charms her as if she is one of the animals, but is her infatuation with him perhaps going a little too far?

BIANCA
Joan Phipson

The first time they see her, Emily and Hubert catch no more than a glimpse of the girl's terrified face as she and her rowing boat loom briefly out of the mist, before it disappears back across the water. But it's a face which haunts them both and they quickly become deeply involved with this strange girl and her mysterious past.

SATURDAY NIGHT
Hunter Davies

What I'm trying to do, is to get off with this girl called Isabella. There, I mentioned her name. I'll have to lie down now. I know, I'll play with my word processor. A bit of harmless fun, like telling you about these wild parties I've just been to, and these girls who just can't control themselves in my presence. It'll kill a bit of time, till my Isabella comes along. Perhaps this Saturday Night . . . ?

THE EMPTY SLEEVE
Leon Garfield

At the age of fourteen, Peter Gannet is apprenticed to a locksmith in Covent Garden but his desperate longing to escape from the insufferable adults around him and go to sea lands him into some dubious undertakings. Before long, the old ship's carpenter's prophecy comes true, when in the locksmith's workroom he meets a phantom with an empty sleeve. A gripping thriller about ghosts, a wall of hands, envy, dishonesty and finally murder!

FOLLOW A SHADOW
Robert Swindells

Tim South is fifteen and finding real life particularly uncomfortable – nothing about it measures up to the colourful fantasy world of his imagination, and hanging out with the tough guys is only making things much worse. However, when he stumbles across a faded picture in the attic of a mysterious young man who looks remarkably like him, Tim becomes obsessed with discovering his identity, sparking off a chilling chain of events that will change his life for ever.

THE TIGER IN THE WELL
Philip Pullman

Sued for divorce when she's never been married, by a man she's never heard of, Sally Lockhart's life is completely uprooted. There seems nothing she can do to prevent the loss of her money, her home, her financial consultancy business, and, most desperately, her dear two-year-old daughter, Harriet.

Sally is a surprising and wonderfully modern heroine, and her fight against unknown and relentless evil in Victorian London makes an exhilarating and unforgettable novel.

MY NAME IS NOT ANGELICA
Scott O'Dell

Raisha was to be married to the proud young chief Konje before they were captured by slave-traders. But on the Caribbean island plantation, Konje soon joins a band of runaways. As the slave revolt grows, so does the harshness of the owners' response, and by the time Raisha is reunited with her lover, the slaves have only one desperate option to take to remain free.

THE ROAD TO MEMPHIS
Mildred D. Taylor

1941 – all America is filled with rumblings of war in Europe and the Pacific. But Cassie Logan has reason to be more concerned with trouble back home in Mississippi. In this new story about the Logan family, Cassie is finishing high school in the city of Jackson and dreaming of college and law school. But no amount of schooling could prepare her for the tense dramas that are about to converge: a quarrel between two young lovers; a black friend's rage at his white tormentors and a white youth's remorse over his part in a violent incident.

Caught up in the centre, Cassie is propelled into three harrowing, exhilarating, unforgettable days that force her to confront the adult world as never before.

SO LONG AT THE FAIR
Hadley Irwin

Joel and Ashley had always been friends, living the rich, fast life. When Ashley commits suicide Joel feels betrayed and desperate – how could she do it? And how can he forget?

DON'T LOOK BEHIND YOU
Lois Duncan

April Corrigan's life really turns into a nightmare when she learns that her father is an undercover agent for the FBI and that his cover is blown. To escape revenge from a drugs gang her father exposes, she and her family are moved from hotel to hotel, until they are finally relocated and given new identities. Then one innocent attempt to regain part of her lost life sparks off a deadly series of events that threatens to destroy her new life too.

THE CRY OF THE WOLF
Melvin Burgess

The Hunter is a fanatic, always on the lookout for rare and exotic animals. Driven by an ambition to wipe out the last English wolves, the Hunter sets out on a savage quest. But he has never before had a prey like Greycub. A wolf that as a cub had been looked after by Ben and his father – a human family. A wolf that knows human needs and weaknesses. A wolf that is determined to survive.